MYSTERY AT SAINT-HILAIRE

by Priscilla Hagon

Mystery at Saint-Hilaire

PRISCILLA HAGON

Illustrated by William Plummer

THE WORLD PUBLISHING COMPANY
CLEVELAND AND NEW YORK

Published by The World Publishing Company
2231 West 110th Street, Cleveland, Ohio 44102
Published simultaneously in Canada by
Nelson, Foster & Scott Ltd.
Library of Congress catalog card number: 68-26971
Text copyright © 1968 by Priscilla Hagon
Illustrations copyright © 1968 by William Plummer
Designed by Jack Jaget

Contents

The Mysterious Letter

I FOUND THE LETTER when I was sorting some library
books. It was thrust between the pages of an adventure
story for children, but, at the time, I gave it scarcely a
second glance because Mr. Wade happened to bustle in
then, looking harassed.

"Could you go and help in the shop, please, Gwenda?
Miss Pritchard isn't feeling well." He ruffled up his thin-
ning hair, gave me a rueful smile, and went out again.

I was in the little back room where we packed and unpacked the library books that were mailed all over France.
Mr. Wade liked to think of his library of English books
as something equivalent to the service Harrod's gives in
Britain. It wasn't anything on that scale, of course, but we
did manage to deal efficiently with a number of distant
members. Wade's British Bookshop was quite an institution
in Paris, and its fame had spread to English-speaking (and
English-reading) people in other parts of France.

So I just glanced at the book I was holding, then ex-
tracted the folded sheet of what looked like a page from
a child's exercise book and thrust it into the big pocket I
happened to have on my pink summer dress. Then I went
out into the shop and helped a British tourist to choose
four Penguin thrillers.

It was early in July and, at the time, I had been living in Paris for six months. It had seemed like a dream at first when Mr. Wade had visited us in London, and, during dinner, had offered me a job. My parents had not liked the idea immediately—"Gwenda's only just eighteen . . . not old enough to live in a foreign country!"—but finally they had agreed that it would undoubtedly be more interesting for me than getting a job in some ordinary London office. I really owed it to my mother, who held the firm belief that young girls should learn to be independent.

"She might be *married* by now," she had argued, when she had had time to think about it.

"Then she'd have a husband to look after her," retorted my father. "However, she's quite a sensible girl, when she doesn't let her imagination get out of hand."

So I had traveled to Paris, already knowing it slightly from two school visits, and Mr. Wade had found me accommodations with some French friends who lived in a charming house on the Butte de Montmartre.

I must admit that I was homesick for a short while, but the spell of Montmartre and the interesting life in the bookshop had gradually made me feel that I had made the right choice. I loved Paris; I had friends; I had always been good at languages and I was soon speaking French, if not like a native, at least pretty well although in Wade's British Bookshop I mostly had to speak my own tongue.

I had friends and I also had Anatole. His parents knew Mr. Wade and, for a short while, I was enchanted to find myself with an attentive French boyfriend. Anatole was a student at the Sorbonne, reasonably clever, not handsome, but with some of the glamour I felt was inevitably attached to a Parisian. For a few weeks in the spring I had imagined myself in love. We had walked by the Seine, in the

Paris squares, and in the little cobblestoned streets of Montmartre. The chestnut trees were in flower all over the city, and the first time Anatole kissed me under a tree on the Champs-Elysées in the Maytime dusk I was enraptured and moved.

But Anatole was possessive, and, I was starting to realize, strangely lacking in humor. My feelings for him had begun to change, although his for me remained the same. And on that day in early July, as I looked out at the traffic in the Rue de Rivoli and the trees of the Tuileries gardens, I was wondering what on earth to do about Anatole. There wasn't anyone else, but I already knew I didn't want to be monopolized.

I could see, with cold common sense, that a lifetime of Anatole wasn't going to be what I wanted. His family were conventional; *he* was conventional. I knew beyond a doubt that he wanted to turn me into a sober housewife, living in a flat in the suburbs and doing the shopping in the most economical places. For Anatole, I had already realized, was a trifle stingy. His parents were well off; he would get a good job when he left the Sorbonne, but he would watch the francs . . . not a doubt of that.

My parents were not rich. For the right man, I knew, I would have watched every centime, but not for Anatole. Oh, definitely not for Anatole! And how to escape?

The day passed. Miss Pritchard—a British spinster who had lived and worked in Paris for many years—went home. I worked hard, only dimly conscious of the summer world outside. When we closed I crossed the Rue de Rivoli and headed for the nearest gate into the Tuileries gardens. I sat on a seat under the trees, relieved that at least Anatole had not been there to meet me. How *awful* to be in love and to find it turn into dust and ashes so soon!

I watched the people pass on the long avenue, hearing the traffic not far away. To my left was the Louvre, to my right the Place de la Concorde. It was quiet and pleasant under the trees and I sank into a dream. Soon I must start on my way home, but I'd wait until the worst of the rush hour on the Métro was over. I always liked the last part of the journey. Sometimes I climbed the different steps that Utrillo painted so often; sometimes I took the funicular, then walked through the Place du Tertre to the

Rue des Saules. Supper wasn't until seven and it was a beautiful day.

I moved and heard a faint crackle in my pocket. So my hand went down and brought out the sheet of exercise paper. I spread it out and saw that it was an unfinished letter, written in a clear, rather childish hand. Not French writing, surely? It somehow had the air of an English schoolgirl. The letter was headed "Le Château de Saint-Hilaire" and was as follows:

Dear David,

I hope you are still enjoying yourself in Vannes. I wish you'd come and see me again. I'm lonely and miserable and I badly need someone to talk to. I'm frightened, Dave. I don't really know why. It's just the atmosphere in this place, I suppose, yet I feel that something is going on. Since the Comte's brother came, nothing has been the same. And one of the fishermen died. . . . Oh, well, that can't really have anything to do with it. But if it wasn't for the child, and the fact that I've little money and nowhere to go, I'd pack my things and leave.

I thought it was so wonderful at first, like something out of a novel, but

And that was all. The letter was unfinished . . . unsigned.

I stared at it, quite unaware of the passing people, of Paris pulsing all around me. Le Château de Saint-Hilaire! Where was that? Was it a real place? But of course it must be, and the letter had been written by a real girl. Not a child, since she referred to a child, though the writing was so unformed.

I folded the letter up carefully and put it in my handbag.

Then I made my way back to the Butte de Montmartre, where my kind hostess (already a very good friend) was cooking a delicious-smelling meal.

"Oh, there you are, Gwenda!" she cried, in the French we always used, for she spoke English badly. "There's a letter for you—from your mother, I think. I put it in your room."

The letter from my mother was warm and chatty, but it contained news that upset me a little. In less than a week's time I had imagined that I should be in London, but Mother wrote that Father was going to Canada on a business trip and she was going with him.

"We mind very much that we shan't see you, Gwenda, dear, but it really is too good an opportunity to miss. The children are going to Aunt May's and I hope you can make some other plans for your holiday. Even stay in Paris, which I know you adore. I'm sure Céleste and her husband wouldn't mind. And Anatole will probably be delighted." Mother knew all about Anatole.

Well, of course I could stay in Paris. Céleste would be delighted. She said I was wonderful company, when her husband was so busy. Or I could go somewhere on my own. There was nothing to stop me from going to another part of France. Mr. Wade paid me well and I hadn't spent the whole of my salary.

I went back to the kitchen to tell Céleste. She raised her dark eyebrows and said:

"Very glad if you don't go, dear child. But you should have a change of scene."

"I'll think about it," I said.

But I found myself thinking instead of that mysterious letter. Who was the girl who was frightened and alone?

How had she come to leave the letter in a children's book? A children's book! I could remember the title—*Adventure in London.*

The next morning, with Miss Pritchard back at her job, I went into the little back room. The book was still there, with a number stamped on the list at the back. A glance at the file told me that the account was in the name of the Comtesse de Saint-Hilaire. The address was Mont Saint-Hilaire, Finistère, Brittany. Further investigation showed me that only children's books had been ordered and the first one had been sent comparatively recently— only four weeks earlier. Miss Pritchard must have sent out the books or else, incredibly, I hadn't noticed the romantic address when I had done so.

Mont Saint-Hilaire! I had an instant vision of that beautiful island on the northern coast of France, Mont Saint-Michel. But there was another island. I had certainly seen pictures of it. There was no causeway leading to it, as there was at Mont Saint-Michel. It rose instead from out of the sea. Mont Saint-Hilaire was, I felt sure, in southern Brittany.

I saw Mr. Wade passing through the shop and went to ask him.

"Please, what do you know about Mont Saint-Hilaire?"

He looked at me kindly.

"A great château on an island. A few cottages. I saw it once when I was staying at Concarneau. The Doumenjous of Saint-Hilaire used to be a rich and well-known family. I have a feeling they've fallen on harder times. Didn't the Comtesse order library books for the child?"

"Yes," I said. "Who is the child?"

He looked vague.

"The Comtesse wrote. Not her own child, of course; I think she's quite elderly. Maybe a grandchild. I suppose they want her to learn English."

"Hard times," I repeated, trying to keep his attention. He was always a vague man in some ways, though he certainly had business abilities. "What do you mean?"

He frowned at me.

"I don't know. I must have heard something. I hope they're not selling the place. I have a feeling there was some tragedy a few months ago. Something out of a Gothic novel."

The unknown writer of the letter had mentioned that it was like something out of a novel. Gothic novels inevitably meant drama and tragedy. But usually with a happy ending.

I would have liked to ask more, but he had gone. So I went back to the library filing system and stared again at the card. There was no more to learn.

It was at that moment, I think, that I knew I had to find out more about Mont Saint-Hilaire—perhaps even go there. I was going to be free in four days' time. I had enough money. Furthermore I had recently started taking color photographs, and I had never seen Brittany. What was to stop me from going exploring?

There was an unknown girl—I was sure it was a girl—in some kind of trouble. She was lonely and frightened. Father always used to say I was a romantic, with too much imagination. I found myself indescribably drawn to that island. I knew that I should never be satisfied unless I went to see for myself. The letter was still in my bag. It must have meant *something*. Maybe the writer of it was wondering at that moment where her letter had gone. Perhaps she thought that someone had found it; someone at the château. Yes, too much imagination.

There was a tourist asking for a copy of an English edition of a book about the French Revolution. I could hear her rather querulous voice, and when I looked out I saw that Miss Pritchard was already serving and trying to answer the other customer at the same time. So I had to go and help, pushing Saint-Hilaire out of my mind.

That evening Anatole was waiting for me when we closed. He had come, he said, to take me out to dinner. But first we would take a walk along the Champs-Elysées. I telephoned Céleste and told her, ruefully, that I would not be home. Céleste laughed, but sympathetically. She, too, thought Anatole without humor. She had heard a good deal about our relationship and was on my side. Anatole was not for me, she had assured me. He needed a nice, serious-minded French girl, one who would soon look plump and dowdy.

We had dinner at a restaurant on the Left Bank. Anatole told me about his studies and never took his eyes off me.

"You are so pretty, Gwenda," he said suddenly. "That very fair hair, the blue eyes. Enchanting! I shall miss you while you're at home in England."

"But—" I began, and then was silent. I wasn't going to London, but Anatole didn't need to know about the change of plans. I felt guilty and mean; of course, I did. But I didn't tell him.

All the time, as we lingered over our coffee, I knew that I was going in search of Mont Saint-Hilaire and the girl who had written the letter. I was going to Brittany alone, adventuring. There was no other plan in my mind.

A Glimpse of
Mont Saint-Hilaire

THE NEXT MORNING was very wet. Clouds of water were
thrown up by passing traffic and the trees in the Tuileries
gardens were extra green in the dismal light. Summer in
Paris!

There were not many people out and it was very quiet
in the shop. Miss Pritchard was arranging some new novels
near the entrance and Mr. Wade was in his office with a
publisher's representative. I had packed up all the library
books ready to be mailed by the young French girl who
was a kind of general help, and, though there were probably things I could have found to do, I gravitated toward
some travel books, including guides, in a back corner.
There were several books about Brittany and I took up one
that seemed to be profusely illustrated.

In a kind of strange excitement, I began to turn the
pages. Under "Morbihan" I suddenly saw the word Vannes
and then a beautiful picture of some old half-timbered
buildings by a little willow-hung river. Above rose the old
city, crowned by the cathedral on a hill. It was a color picture; there was a blue sky and very white clouds. It looked
enchanting.

The letter had been addressed to someone called David,
who seemed to be in Vannes. The girl's boyfriend? A

brother? I couldn't possibly guess, but it must be someone she trusted.

I went on turning the pages until I came to the chapter under the heading of "Finistère." There was a picture of Concarneau, with the *ville close* (the old walled town) on an island in the harbor—an island fortress, beautiful and romantic. There was another picture showing a narrow old street overhung with the blue nets of the fishermen, and a third of old women in wonderful Breton costumes, with high, elaborate *coiffes* on their heads.

"In Concarneau, during the Festival of the Blue Nets—"

Fascinating, but where was Mont Saint-Hilaire? I looked at the index and then found the page. There was a picture that seemed to stop my heart, of sweeping sands, rocks, and a small, almost conical, island. There were cottages at the lowest point and the whole was crowned by a château with towers and pinnacles. It looked like something out of a fairy tale.

"Mont Saint-Hilaire, unlike its northern counterpart, Mont Saint-Michel, is surprisingly little visited," I read. "It is on a remote part of the coast and the road approaches are narrow and bad. Buses are infrequent and there is no causeway to give easy access to the island. At low tide it is possible to walk over the sands from a point a little east of the fishing village of Port Guenil; otherwise it is necessary to hire a boat. The Château de Saint-Hilaire, originally a fortress, then a monastery, has been inhabited by the Doumenjou family for three hundred years. It has many interesting features, but is never shown to the public.

"Port Guenil's only claim to fame is that it has one of the ancient Breton festivals in the middle of July, when the fishing boats and nets are blessed. But it is in no way on the scale of other *pardons* and festivals that take place in southern Brittany.

"Inland is a ring of standing stones, not so fine as those at Carnac. They are called *Les Jeunes Filles*, and the legend bears a close resemblance to the one relating to a group of similar stones in Cornwall, England. Young girls were dancing under the moon and were frozen into stone. . . ."

"You might come and serve, Gwenda!" called Miss Pritchard, and I saw that the shop had been invaded by two or three dripping tourists, presumably driven out of their hotels in search of something to read.

I obeyed, but my mind was still occupied with Mont Saint-Hilaire.

That evening, as Céleste and I sat over our coffee (her husband, Jean, was at a business dinner), I told her something of my plans, though I didn't mention the mysterious letter. Céleste looked a little doubtful at first. For a French-woman her ideas were pretty modern when it came to the freedom of young girls, but I could see that she didn't wholly like the idea of my wandering alone in Brittany.

"Are you sure your mother would like it, Gwenda?" she asked, after a few moments.

I laughed.

"Honestly, I don't think she'd mind at all. She'd probably say that if I can cope with Paris I can cope with Breton villages."

"But they don't always speak French, so I believe," she said. "I've never been to Brittany, but I gather the old Breton tongue is still much spoken, particularly by the older people."

"Then maybe I can prove something I've always wanted to know," I remarked. "My mother is Welsh, as I told you, and, as a child, I spent a lot of time with my Welsh grand-mother in a village by the sea. I still remember quite a lot of Welsh, and they say that when the Breton onion sellers go over to Wales they can make themselves understood. The two languages, and Cornish, all come from the same source. They're Celtic . . . Gaelic."

"Very interesting," said Céleste. "Myself, I don't care for primitive lands, and I think Brittany can still be quite primitive. You had better go to the main towns and villages. Otherwise, the sanitation—" She shuddered.

"I thought of going to Port Guenil," I said. "For a start, anyway. I want to take pictures, and Mont Saint-Hilaire sounds fascinating."

Céleste looked as though she'd never heard of Mont Saint-Hilaire, and I must confess I felt a little guilty. I was going in search of a mystery and Céleste—perhaps even my mother—could hardly approve of that. I also felt guilty about Anatole, but I went on:

"Céleste, dear, I haven't told Anatole. He thinks I'm still going to London. I don't want him to follow me. I've got to *do* something about Anatole. It will give me time to think."

Céleste laughed and shrugged.

"You simply tell him that you don't want to see him any more."

"But I can't hurt his feelings. Though I suppose I'm bound to, sooner or later."

"He will eventually find the right woman. No, I won't tell him. But you are to telephone every few days, Gwenda. Give me an address."

"I'll do that," I promised.

I still had to find out how to get to Port Guenil, so the

next day, during my lunch hour, I went to a travel agent's office. The result was a great deal of literature about Brittany—more pictures of romantic towns and people in beautiful costumes—and a very small folder giving the times of buses from Quimperlé to Port Guenil. They only went three times a week and seemed mainly planned to take the people of Port Guenil to civilization. Luckily there was one on the afternoon of the day I intended to travel to Brittany.

A mystery, perhaps. But it was more than that. My imagination was strangely fired by thoughts of Mont Saint-Hilaire. Not since I had yearned to get to Paris had I been so drawn by a place. I took one of the books about Brittany home with me, with Mr. Wade's permission, and soaked myself in the stories of village *pardons* (religious festivals), ancient cathedrals and even more ancient standing stones.

A strange, bleak land. . . . But it drew me as Wales had done as a child. Perhaps just because I thought it would be like Wales in some ways. Without the mountains, of course. Well, probably more like Cornwall. At all events, I couldn't wait to get there.

I begged Mr. Wade not to tell Anatole I had gone to Brittany and he laughed, crinkling up his eyes in the nice way he had.

"If that young man comes I don't know anything. I've lived in France for twenty years, but I still prefer British young men."

"Frenchmen aren't all like Anatole," I said.

I managed to avoid Anatole until my last evening in Paris. When he telephoned I told him I was busy and he seemed annoyed, but didn't insist. But on my last evening there he was waiting for me in the Rue de Rivoli.

My heart sank, because I felt very guilty indeed by then, but I told myself I wasn't going to explain my change of plans.

Anatole seemed so pleased to see me that it seemed terribly ungrateful to want to escape. I looked at him covertly while we ate. He wasn't bad looking; he had nice brown hair, a good nose and he was well-groomed for a student. But his mouth was too small and too tight. In five years' time Anatole would be a humorless husband and father, grumbling over household bills. I didn't love him; that was the whole trouble.

"I shall miss you so much, Gwenda," he said, as we parted in the Rue des Saules. He had insisted on taking me all the way home. "When will you be back?"

"In about two weeks," I told him, my hand on the old iron gate that gave access to a tiny courtyard.

"Wait! You haven't given me your parents' address. Hampstead, London, I know, but—"

"Oh, don't bother to write," I said quickly. "I wouldn't have time to answer. Good night, Anatole, and thank you."

I whisked through the gate, catching a last glimpse of his hurt face. I felt mean, but soon my thoughts had gone back to Mont Saint-Hilaire.

It was only as the train was pulling out of Rennes the next day that the thought occurred to me that the letter I had found might be an old one. I had been taking it for granted that it had been written recently, then somehow left in the children's book when it was returned to Paris. The book had just arrived on the day I found the letter.

But suppose it had been written months before and had only been used by someone to mark the place? Or idly picked up and for some reason thrust between the pages?

I took out the letter and looked at it. The paper was clean and the only creases were the ones where it had been folded. No, I was sure there was a girl on Mont Saint-Hilaire who really was lonely and afraid. Some tragedy, Mr. Wade had said. But he was speaking of the past; not of something that had happened very recently.

I might not find out anything—there might be nothing much to find out. But I was already in Brittany; I could see rather poor fields and farms, and great banks of gorse. The sky was blue and the people working in the fields looked hot. There was no sign of the sea.

It was quite a long journey, and by the time the train stopped at Quimperlé I was very warm, thirsty, and impatient. I was also terribly afraid I was going to miss the bus. And there wasn't another until Friday!

I had packed most of my things in a rucksack, to Céleste's amusement, but I also had my handbag and small suitcase. I have only the haziest recollection of that first visit to Quimperlé. Old houses . . . a pretty river . . . the streets burning in the late afternoon sun.

I caught the bus with five minutes to spare. It was a small, shabby one, not like most of the French buses, and it was only half full. There were two or three people who looked like tourists, but the rest were mostly old women in black, with shopping baskets. One wore a very small, neat *coiffe* on her white hair and looked about eighty. There was a strong smell of onions from the basket nearest to me.

Presently we went lurching away out of the town, with me hot, more thirsty than ever, and feeling very alien, clinging to the seat in front. I could hear snatches of a language that certainly wasn't French, but the two old women were not near enough for me to distinguish any words.

After a time the roads grew very narrow, with high earthen banks covered with blazing gorse. Its nutty fragrance came through the open windows and mingled with the smell of onions. We stopped occasionally at tiny gray villages, putting down two or three passengers, never taking anyone on. Then I saw a signpost that said: "Port Guenil: 10 kilomètres." Soon I would be there!

Once, rounding a bend, we nearly collided with a shabby car. It was driven by a young man, who stopped abruptly, backed close against the gorse-covered bank, and sat there, frowning. Then suddenly he smiled and raised his hand in apology, though actually they had *both* been going dangerously fast and it was a miracle there hadn't been an accident.

The bus driver, not to be placated (he clearly thought he owned the road), yelled something in French, but I only caught the words: "Monsieur Doumenjou."

Doumenjou! Of Mont Saint-Hilaire? As we eased past I tried to get a better glimpse of the young man. He was dark-haired and very much suntanned. He wore an open-necked blue shirt and I noticed long brown hands on the wheel. He had looked different when he smiled, but I was left with an impression of frowning concentration, as though his thoughts as he drove hadn't been pleasant ones. Mr. Wade hadn't mentioned a son, only a grandchild. Perhaps the young man was the child's brother.

The sky suddenly seemed even brighter and higher, suggesting that at last the sea wasn't far away. We shot past some large stones in a field, close to a tiny, wind-blown wood. Stones in a ring, ancient and brooding. Perhaps *Les Jeunes Filles* . . . the young girls who, as legend had it, had been turned to stone in some unimaginable past age. They had an eerie look, even under the blue, blue sky. I felt I wouldn't like them in the dark. How

Céleste would have laughed! She was entirely practical.

There were only six people left in the bus. Even the tourists had left; I'd seen them approaching what seemed to be a remote inn. They had strong walking shoes and seemed to be speaking German.

At last we came in sight of the sea; we were rushing along a lane only a stone's throw from black rocks and silver-white sand. But there wasn't much sand, for the tide was high. Away to the left, washed by blue water, I caught my first glimpse of Mont Saint-Hilaire. And oh! It *was* as beautiful as a dream and looked as unattainable!

In the clear light I could see gray-roofed cottages climbing the slope, to end under frowning bastions. On the highest point of the island, rising above the ancient lower walls, were the towers and turrets of the château.

I saw it and knew that I really was under a kind of spell. The unknown place had filled my thoughts for days. Now I saw it in reality, looking like a place out of a romantic medieval story. Much must have happened there during the long centuries; anything, I felt, could happen now. And if there really was an English girl over there, alone and scared. . . .

As we drove at dangerous speed into the narrow, sun-baked streets of Port Guenil, I tried to force my mind back to practical matters. I had to find somewhere to stay; that was the first thing. Perhaps some of the whitewashed cottages took visitors. There might even be an inn.

I barely repressed a cry of alarm as the driver swung the bus almost onto a narrow jetty. For a moment, as he backed fiercely and then turned his vehicle around, I thought we were going to end up in the harbor, among all the brightly colored boats. But the old fishermen sitting smoking their pipes didn't even raise an eyebrow.

I grabbed my rucksack and swung it onto one shoulder. Then I took my little suitcase in the other hand and bumped my way out of the bus. The strong sea smell assailed me and the light was dazzling.

I stood there blinking, staring out to Mont Saint-Hilaire. The next moment a hand had taken my suitcase and I felt a jerk on my rucksack strap. I swung around to look into the wrinkled face of an elderly man. He wore sea boots, blue trousers, and a fisherman's jersey. Across the front of the jersey were the words "Mont Saint-Hilaire."

"You are the English mademoiselle," he said in French that was rough and not easy to understand. "Come with me. The boat is waiting."

"But—" I said, blank with astonishment.

He had already taken my suitcase and rucksack and was hurrying along the jetty. I ran after him, with protests rising on my tongue. "But I'm not! I mean—" My beautiful Parisian French seemed to have deserted me. I found I had spoken in English.

At the foot of some moss-covered steps was a white launch. Quite a big boat, but shabby, needing a new coat of paint. She was called *La Rose de Saint-Hilaire*.

The old man was already on board. He was holding up his hand to me, smiling with tobacco-stained lips.

"Madame la Comtesse expects you."

Later I could never explain why I let it happen. I suppose I could have insisted on getting my luggage back. I could have convinced him easily enough that Madame la Comtesse could not possibly expect me.

Instead I jumped down into the boat.

At the Château

As we left the picturesque little harbor the sea wind lifted my hair and I felt cool and renewed. I think I seriously doubted my own identity. Perhaps I really was some other girl, who had every right to be going out to the island.

Or perhaps—and my heart gave a slight lurch—it was some plot. Maybe they knew I had found the mysterious letter and were making sure that they had me in their clutches.

But I could hear Céleste saying: "You read too many romantic stories, Gwenda. Such things don't happen."

It certainly was nonsense. I had mentioned the letter to no one, and no one could possibly know I had found it. So someone else must have been expected, and when I reached Mont Saint-Hilaire it was going to be very difficult and embarrassing. But at least I would have seen the island quickly and when I slept that night I would have real memories of it to haunt my dreams.

It lay perhaps half a mile outside the harbor and a little to the left. At low tide, I assumed, the inhabitants would walk across the sands to arrive on the outskirts of Port Guenil. As we drew nearer I could see that there

26

was a tiny harbor on Mont Saint-Hilaire, with more gaily painted boats. Blue nets were festooned over posts and there was smoke rising from the chimneys of the tiny, crowding cottages.

The château looked impregnable on its high rocks. It certainly ought to house men in armor or monks (and had done both, apparently, in the past). I couldn't imagine a modern family living out their ordinary lives in such a place. But it was so.

My boatman hadn't spoken another word. He was some distance from me, at the controls. I planned, nervous at last, to explain just as soon as we landed and to ask him to take me straight back to Port Guenil.

I did try.

"Monsieur, I'm not the girl you were expecting. It must all be a mistake and I'm very sorry."

But he didn't even listen. I began to think he was probably deaf. He simply reached up and dumped my suitcase and rucksack on the steps above us, then climbed out and reached for my hand. He did say something in his rough, unfamiliar French. It sounded like: "The rest of your baggage is coming later?"

"No," I said. "No. And madame doesn't expect me—"

But the next moment he had shouldered my rucksack, taken my suitcase and, with a jerk of his head, indicated that I was to follow him.

I looked around for someone with more sense, or better ears, but there was no one at all. The cobblestones around the harbor were hot and empty in the sun; there was no longer any wind.

We climbed some shallow steps and walked through a narrow alleyway between cottages. Then there was a tiny climbing street, lined with flat-fronted gray houses. In one doorway an old woman sat in a rocking chair, knitting. She gave me a quick, curious glance and murmured something. Probably just a greeting. I had forgotten all about wanting to compare the Breton tongue with Welsh. I doubt if I would have been capable of it then.

The sound of a radio came from one cottage, a baby was crying in another. The only other sign of life was a beautiful black cat sunning himself on a doorstep.

The old man went fast and I panted after him. The way was steep, the sun was hot on my back, and I was filled with a great mixture of emotions. Exasperation . . . excitement . . . nervousness . . . perhaps a faint touch of fear because Madame la Comtesse was going to be terribly annoyed. How on earth was I going to make her understand why I ever got into the boat at all? It was a ridiculous situation and I should never have gotten myself into it.

We were by then quite high and were faced with a flight of stone steps. The old man paused to rest and I swung thankfully around. The view was glorious. I looked over the old rooftops to the sea and the sweep of the mainland coast. I could see Port Guenil, bright in the sun, and—some distance away to the west—a great rocky headland. If my camera hadn't been in my suitcase I think I would have taken a picture. I would at least have had *that*, I thought, as we went on.

Up and up until we came to a kind of gatehouse and some thick wooden doors, tight shut. But there was a small door in the right-hand big one and it swung open suddenly to reveal a little girl. A child of about eleven, I thought, but very small, thin, and plain. She wore a blue cotton dress, slightly too large for her. I noticed, though, in those brief moments while she stared at me, that she had very fine eyes; big gray eyes with long dark lashes.

"Oh, you have come!" she cried, in English. "I am so glad! It has been so lonely. *Grandmère* doesn't like to play and Sebastien has gone away. Mostly he has been out fishing, anyway. *Grandmère* is not well, you see. And—"

My escort broke into speech and the child answered in the same tongue. Then, at last, I fully heard the words and I was startled to find that they had a certain famil-

iarity. I didn't understand every word, but I got his mean-
ing. He had asked her to take me to her grandmother,
as he wanted to go off fishing.

The child nodded and gestured, and then another person appeared behind her, an old woman in black. She
took my luggage without a word, and, though I tried to
protest, set off, carrying it easily. I looked helplessly at
the child.

"The poor little girl!" I thought. "She thinks I've come
to keep her company."

I didn't know how to explain, and, in any case, the too
long blue dress was following the shabby black one. I
followed, vaguely noticing that we were in a sheltered
garden behind the ramparts. There were some very fine
roses and their scent filled the air. Beyond the garden
the château rose dark and brooding. There were steps up
to a massive oak door, which stood partly open.

The child suddenly paused and waited for me.

"You are called Mary Smithson, isn't that so? Me, I am
Guennola Doumenjou. You think I speak good English?
At school I learned some and then Sara taught me much
more. Together we read the English storybooks. You will
read with me, please?"

I have two little sisters. At that time one of them was
just eleven, a gay, assured child. Guennola had an air
that I hoped neither of them would ever have. She looked
lost, forlorn, not very healthy. Her expression was definitely unchildlike.

I felt worse than ever. Her name had given me a jolt,
for it was very like mine. My real name is Gwendolen,
though Mother always said it was too long and she didn't
like "Gwen." It was extraordinary to find this Breton child
almost sharing my name, and I think the fact may have

had some bearing on the decision I was soon to make. A strange feeling that fate *meant* me to be there.

"Guennola," I said, after quite a long pause, "I'm not Mary Smithson. It's all been a mistake. I'm so sorry."

She stood very still, looking at me gravely.

"I do not mind what your name is. I like you. You are very pretty."

"But, you see, I can't stay. The boatman wouldn't listen to me."

"Oh yes, please stay!" she begged, coming forward to take my hand. "Come to *Grandmère*. She is most anxious for me to have company. *Mon grandpère* doesn't wish it so much. I heard him say that there was no need for another girl."

The old woman had disappeared with my luggage. I followed Guennola toward the great doorway. Something had become clear in my mind. There had been a girl called Sara, who read books with Guennola; books from Wade's library. Sara had been frightened and she had gone. But why? And *where* had she gone?

"Where is Sara?" I asked, as we entered a vast dim hall.

But Guennola didn't seem to have heard. She rapidly led the way up a very grand staircase and along a wide dark corridor. There were paintings on the paneled walls. It was a house, after all, though darker and more splendid than most. Yet it was shabby, too. There was a feeling— even a smell—a slight decay, and, as I followed the child into a big room, I was dimly aware that the beautiful carpet had seen much better days.

The room was surprisingly light. It was flooded with sunshine and the reflection of the sea. It was a drawing room, and, by the window, sat an elderly woman. With an unreasonable sense of shock, I saw that she was quite an ordinary-looking woman. She was, in fact, dowdy. She wore a navy-blue dress and her white hair was screwed up in a knot. She had a cane beside her chair and looked like anyone's grandmother out of a slightly earlier age. Grandmothers nowadays usually seem to be very smartly dressed and brisk.

She didn't rise, but sat staring at us, and there was an expression of great surprise on her face. In that moment I saw that she had eyes like Guennola's.

The child was chattering—in French now.

"*Grandmère,* here is Mary Smithson. But she says that isn't her name. She says it is a mistake and she can't stay. Please tell her to stay."

The Comtesse looked more startled than ever. I went up to her quickly, also speaking in French.

"Truly I am sorry. I came from Paris to Port Guenil, hoping to find somewhere to stay for a few days. And the boatman took my luggage. I couldn't make him understand."

"He's very deaf and rather stupid," she said. "Then who are you, my dear?" She had a very attractive voice.

"My name is Gwenda Maitland. I work in Paris—in Wade's British Bookshop—but my home is in London. My parents have gone to Canada, and I couldn't go home for my holiday. I thought I would come and explore Brittany and take some color photographs."

"The boatman thought you were the new girl . . . the new companion for Guennola," she said. "But just in these last few minutes there has been a telephone call. The wretched girl, Mary Smithson, has taken another job. She'd been with a family in Rennes and wanted a change. She had good references and I thought she would be all right. But she, apparently, thought better of coming to

Mont Saint-Hilaire. Young girls nowadays like to be near towns, where there are things to do. I told her she might have let me know earlier, but it seems she lacked the courage."

Guennola had followed this exchange with a downcast air. Her face looked so small and pale that I felt worse than ever.

"I really am sorry," I said. "I'll go now, if you will have my luggage brought back to me. Surely someone will take me back to Port Guenil?"

"Wait!" she said. She might be dowdy, but she had quite an imperious air. "I can see that Guennola likes you. You came to this part of Brittany because it attracted you. Would it perhaps attract you to stay here for a while?"

I was staggered, and felt I must have been dreaming. To stay on the island—to live in that romantic stronghold.

"I—I don't know," I stammered. "It could only be for two weeks. I have to go back to my job."

"To Wade's British Bookshop, you said? I have books sent for Guennola from there."

"Yes, madame, I know," I told her.

Guennola was at my side, holding my hand.

"Oh, please stay! It will be such fun. I will show you everything. We will read and even do lessons. I shall not mind lessons with you."

"She really quite likes her lessons," said the Comtesse. "But the doctor said that she must not be taxed. She was at boarding school and was taken ill there. Run along, Guennola! See that Miss Maitland's room looks nice. It seems possible that she will stay for a while."

Guennola gave us both a very unchildlike look. I was suddenly aware that I was to be told something and that she knew what it would be. Then she smiled warmly at

me, said: "Oh, mademoiselle, please do stay!" and obediently walked away.

"She is an orphan," the Comtesse said quietly. "We
had a terrible tragedy here last November. Her father and
mother—our only son and his wife—had been to Paris
and were crossing from Port Guenil in a rough sea. The
boat's engine apparently failed and no one saw that they
were in trouble. The weather was very bad, visibility poor.
They drifted onto sharp rocks over near Pointe Noire.
Their bodies were recovered days later."

"Oh, how terrible!" I cried.

"The boat had been left for them and Jacques was at
the controls, but he knew the crossing as well as anyone
on the island." Her voice shook slightly. "It was a bad
time. Guennola was away at school and we thought it
best to keep her there. They were all so kind to her. But,
in the spring, she was very ill. She's so sensitive, poor little
one. So now she remains here, but no governess will stay.
They don't like to be cut off from amusements. Sara, who
was here until a few days ago, was just an *au pair* girl,
but quite well educated. She—"

The door opened and an elderly man came in. He
looked very much older than his wife. A tall man, with
a worn but still handsome face. He looked anything but
pleased.

"Marie, what's this wild story Guennola tells me? The
one girl isn't coming, but another is here instead." He
was looking at me with disfavor; almost with downright
unfriendliness. Yet I thought perhaps it was just that he
had other things on his mind.

His wife explained rapidly and there was an element
of pleading in her voice.

"Gwenda could stay for two weeks. It would be someone for Guennola. She oughtn't to be alone so much, or chattering with the fishermen. She needs real company and I—You know I'm not up to it."

He looked as though he would like to argue. Instead, he said: "She has no references."

"You could telephone Mr. Wade," I said. I knew that I wouldn't be able to bear it if I had to go away after all. "It's five-fifteen. He'll still be at the shop."

"Yes, I'll do that," the Comtesse said eagerly.

The Comte surveyed me. Unlike his wife he had a great deal of presence, and I found myself in awe of him, even a little afraid. But probably I wouldn't need to see him very much.

"You always get your own way, my dear," he said to his wife. "Put a call through to Paris by all means." Then he turned on his heel and went out.

I had the feeling that there was far more than I understood. For a moment the Comtesse looked after him with a very strange expression on her face. A heart-rending look, full of doubt and grief. Then it was gone and she reached for the telephone.

I stood by the window, staring out at that superb view. Paris seemed unimaginably far away, but very soon I knew that she was speaking to Mr. Wade. I could picture him in his office, rumpling up his hair. He must be very surprised to be talking to the Comtesse of Saint-Hilaire about me. But apparently what he said was satisfactory, for she hung up and smiled at me.

"Your Mr. Wade likes you. What he said was very complimentary. So you'll stay, my dear? It may be rather unconventional, but Guennola needs someone so badly."

It *was* unconventional. I wondered suddenly what my parents would say. The Comtesse could give *me* no refer-

ences. But they were one of the old families of France.
The child undoubtedly needed a companion and it seemed
as though fate had sent me there in place of Mary Smithson. I had not much liked the Comte's manner and his
obvious reluctance to accept me, but I did like and pity
Guennola. For the time being, though it may be hard to
believe, I had wholly forgotten that a hint of mystery and
fear had brought me to the island.

The Comtesse rang a bell and the same old woman who
had taken my luggage appeared.

"This is Kérity," my hostess said. "She was born on
Mont Saint-Hilaire and has worked at the château since
she was fourteen. She speaks French, though you may
find her accent unfamiliar. She will see that you are comfortable."

I was about to explain about Breton and Welsh when
I realized that I had been dismissed. The old woman led
me along the corridor and up another flight of stairs. My
room, when we came to it, was large, overfurnished, and
shabby, but there was a vase of red roses and a marvelous
view of the sea. Guennola was sitting on the bed.

When the old woman had gone I began to unpack
hastily. I wondered if I would have enough clothes for
life at the château. Not that the appearance of either Guennola or her grandmother suggested that there was much
dressing up.

Bending over my suitcase I asked suddenly, interrupt-
ing the child's chatter about books:

"What happened to Sara? Why did she go?"

"Oh, poor Sara!" The big gray eyes opened very wide.
"She fell down the stairs of the West Tower. She is in
Quimperlé Hospital with a broken leg. The doctor said
it was a miracle she wasn't killed."

My heart leaped sickeningly. The girl who had written that mysterious, disturbing letter! She had felt that something was going on.

I stood up and stared at the child in the blue dress. The room was warm, for the sunlight was pouring in, but I felt a chill of fear.

Unanswered Questions

"How did it happen?" I asked, striving to make my voice sound ordinary. The child looked so very tense it was clear that the memory of the accident upset her. Poor Guennola, she must feel that tragedy was ever present.

"I do not really know," she said slowly. "I didn't see Sara, you understand, after the accident. I was with *Grandmère* at the time. She wished to hear me read, since Sara had told her how well I was progressing with the English books. Sara loved to paint. She was painting a picture from the top of the tower. The stairs are very old, you know, and she never wore the sensible shoes."

It might have been just that. A careless movement, a heel missing the uneven step. But it shook me badly, and, for a wild moment, I thought of throwing all my things back into my suitcase and rucksack and returning to Port Guenil at once. Or as soon as a boat would take me there.

The child seemed to sense something of what was going on in my mind. She sprang off the bed, looking at me with appeal.

"Oh, please! You will stay? I cannot bear it if you go away."

We almost shared a name and I was wrung with pity at her abrupt and terrible loss of both parents. Also, there was a strong element of curiosity, and this far exceeded my fear.

I knew that if I went away from Mont Saint-Hilaire I would always feel dissatisfied, robbed of something. Almost certainly, though, there was nothing in the mystery. I would spend two weeks at the château, lost in a kind of dream world, and then go back to my ordinary life.

"Of course I'm staying," I assured Guennola, and put the last of my things away.

After that I took a bath in a vast, old-fashioned bathroom at the end of the corridor, put on a clean dress and made up my face. Guennola remained in my room, after asking politely if I minded.

While I was doing my face she mentioned Sebastien again.

"Is he your brother?" I asked. "And does he drive an old red car? Because, if he does, I think I saw him on the road to Quimperlé."

"Not my brother," Guennola said sadly. "I have no brothers or sisters. He is my cousin, quite distant; but I have known him all my life. When he was younger he used to spend a great deal of time here. Now he's twenty-three; that is really very old in some ways. Yes, he drives an old red car. He has gone to visit a friend in Brest for a day or two. At least I think that's where he has gone. I heard him asking for a Brest telephone number. You thought he was nice, yes?"

I visualized the young man I had seen so briefly. How could I say if he was "nice"? He certainly had an interesting face, but he was either naturally ill-tempered or he had been worried about something.

"Where does he work?" I asked, surprised that I was really curious about the unknown Sebastien.

"In Paris, and his parents live there also. It was a lovely surprise," said Guennola eagerly. Her face looked quite different when she was animated. "He came quite suddenly two weeks ago, asking if he could spend his holidays here. Last year I didn't see him, because he went to Switzerland. I love Sebastien. He is very nice to me, but he likes to fish. Always out in the boats. Me, I do not like the boats any more."

I looked at her, suddenly not sure of what to say. Should I talk to her about the terrible tragedy or not?

"Your grandmother told me," I said finally. "I'm sorry, Guennola. It was very dreadful."

She didn't cry, or even display any great emotion, though her face looked smaller than ever.

"Sometimes I don't think I like Mont Saint-Hilaire any more. But there is nowhere else to live. Sara said the only way was to get used to the idea that the sea is sometimes cruel. But often I wish I could go far away. To Paris, perhaps, where there is no sea, only the river Seine."

"Paris is lovely," I said. "But you belong to Mont Saint-Hilaire."

"But it may happen that we all go away," she said slowly. "We're so poor, you see. *Grandpère* minds very much. Once I heard him talking to *Grandmère*. He said he would do anything to keep Mont Saint-Hilaire in the family—to make it safe for me. Then he said: 'But as far as I can see, in five years or less I shall have to sell. How will you like to live in a flat in Paris, Marie?'"

I didn't know what to say. It seemed that Mr. Wade had been right. But, after three hundred years, a flat in Paris. . . .

Finally I said quietly:

"All the great families seem to be losing their money. But it can't, surely, be as bad as that?"

"I think perhaps yes. We are very poor."

The old woman, Kérity, came then to say that a meal was waiting for us both. It was a great relief to know that I didn't have to dine with Guennola's grandparents. I felt that I had coped with quite enough for one day. I thought, as I followed the child downstairs, that I had never experienced a more adventurous and extraordinary day in my whole life.

The meal, which was a very simple one, was served in a small, rather dark room that looked toward a narrow courtyard and the great stone bastions. We were waited on briefly by a very young girl, who seemed shy and rather overcome by her duties. Then we were left alone, except for the presence of three cats; one ginger, one black, and the third tortoise-shell. Guennola said there were no dogs at the château; in fact, there wasn't a single dog on the island.

"*Grandpère* loves cats, but he has never liked dogs, so no one keeps any. They are all our tenants, you see, and must obey."

Guennola said this very matter-of-factly and clearly saw nothing unusual in it. But the calm statement filled me with a wave of amazement. I felt, for a few moments, as though I really must be dreaming. I could *not* be in a château on an island that was still feudal! It was a dream, a piece of staggering unreality.

Then, as my mind began to work again, I smiled with wry amusement, trying to imagine the Comte and his wife leading everyday lives in a flat in Paris, far from the island where they were almost royalty.

"You find it funny?" Guennola asked, puzzled. "Me, I am sometimes a little sorry. I would like a dog of my own. A black poodle with a red ribbon."

"Not funny, no," I said. "Just strange, in these days, that your grandfather's word is law."

"Sara said that," she remarked, helping herself to some more of the delicious crusty bread. "Sara thought it was all very strange. She said it was—was a shock to her system, after living in a little house in Ealing."

My heart warmed to Sara, who must have felt some of my own emotions. And now she was alone and possibly in pain in a French hospital. I wondered if anyone was visiting her; if the young man in Vannes, or any relatives, had been informed. Somehow I had to go and see Sara quite soon.

"What is Sara like?" I asked, and Guennola frowned, obviously finding it a hard question.

"Nice," she said finally. "She is not, I think, a very happy person, but this made me like her more. She said she never had much fun when she was young, so she made up stories and later tried to paint."

Made up stories! So could the letter have been part of a story, perhaps? But it had *looked* like a proper letter.

"Has she a boyfriend?"

Guennola pushed her hair out of her eyes.

"I do not think so. She mentioned only her brother. His name is David and he is working just now in Vannes."

So that much had been real. I was more curious about Sara than ever.

"Do you ever go far on the mainland?" I asked. "Wouldn't you like to visit Sara?"

"We keep a car over at Port Guenil," Guennola said slowly. "And also, of course, there is the bus. The car is not much used, as only *Grandpère* drives it. Oh, yes, I would *love* to see Sara, but when I asked *mon grand-*

père he said that she was in too much pain to be visited by one who would chatter. I promised that I would be very quiet, but still he said no. He told me he had made all arrangements for her comfort and that the English aunt has been informed. But she is old. Sara is like me— an orphan."

I made no reply and she went on in a kind of burst:

"No one is the same these days. *Grandpère* doesn't talk to me as much as he used to; I think he is worried about money. And *Grandmère* is not well; her bad leg gives her much pain, I think. And even Sebastien seemed different after a while. Me, I don't understand, but it all started when Oncle Pierre came."

I remembered that sentence from Sara's mysterious letter: "Nothing has been the same since the Comte's brother came." It was a curious coincidence that she and the child should use almost the same phrase.

"Your Uncle Pierre? Is he here now?"

"No. He was only here for a few days. I do not like Oncle Pierre, and he and *mon grandpère* have never gotten along." She said this as though it were something she had heard. "But this time they seemed—They talked together much. Once I heard them quarreling. Then, the day after Sara's accident, he went away and I was very glad."

"And then one of the fishermen died—" Sara had said in her letter. But I couldn't ask Guennola about that. The food had helped, but I was very tired, still partly held in that sense of unreality.

I was glad when Guennola's bedtime came, at eight-thirty. She went to say good night to her grandparents and I saw her into bed. Kérity came with a glass of hot milk.

Apparently Guennola always had it last thing. The old woman said in her rough French that the child did not sleep very well and it helped.

"You also would like something when you sleep, Mademoiselle?" she asked. "The lemonade? Or tea? The English like tea."

Supper had been early. I might be hungry.

"Cold milk, please," I said. "And perhaps some cookies, Kérity."

"They will be in your room each night," the old woman promised. "The milk will keep cold in a Thermos bottle. Here we have the refrigerator." She said it with great pride. "It is old, but it works."

I wandered away down the long dim corridor. It was still daylight outside and I felt that I needed some air. I found my way to the great front door and out into the garden. The roses smelled more sweetly than ever and the bastions looked black against the evening sky. The little door in the big one was still open and I went through it and sat on the steps, staring down at the little houses and the curve of the harbor. The tide was out now and the great swirling sands stretched between the island and the mainland. I was so tired that I could hardly think at all. Paris seemed very far away and I could hardly remember Anatole.

I yawned and decided that bed was the only place. In the corridor on the first floor I passed Monsieur le Comte. He seemed, at first, not to see me, then he said: *"Bon soir, mademoiselle."*

I undressed, washed briefly, then took a last look out of the window. The sunset was dying now. The whole world was washed in soft pink.

I got into bed and pulled the bedclothes over me, then

saw the Thermos and the plate of cookies. I drank the milk and ate one cookie, and after that I turned out the light and sank down on the soft bed. I never ate after I had cleaned my teeth, but tonight was different. I didn't care.

On the edge of sleep, pictures came into my mind. Sebastien sitting in the red car . . . myself, helpless in the hands of fate (or my own curiosity), heading across the summer sea to the island . . . Guennola in her blue dress . . . the Comte's lined face. Sara—*Had* someone pushed Sara? Or was the whole thing a figment of an unhappy girl's imagination? There was certainly not a very cheerful atmosphere at the château, but there had been tragedy there not long ago and there certainly seemed a shortage of money. My own eyes told me so, quite without Guennola's remarks. Everything was so shabby; there seemed a lack of domestic help. Apart from Kérity and the young girl I had seen only a very old man, wearing a black apron. That must be quite enough to worry the owners of Mont Saint-Hilaire, and might well worry the brother, too.

Céleste's sensible face floated into my mind. What on earth would she say if she could see me as part of this extraordinary household? And what would Anatole think?

I slept, without finding any answers to my questions.

Seeing Sara

I WAS AWAKENED by Guennola the next morning. It was nearly eight o'clock and the sunlight was lying on the sea and the great beach I could see from my window. The tide had been up in the night and was going out again.

I awoke quickly and completely and knew full well where I was, though there was still a stab of amazement in the realization.

Guennola, wearing a red and white dress this time, came in carefully balancing a tray of tea. Behind her came the three cats I had seen last night and two very handsome striped ones.

"Because the English so like the morning tea," she said, more cheerfully than I had yet heard her speak. She plumped herself down on the bed and watched me drink the familiar French liquid. Sometimes I longed for a real English pot of tea, without those wretched little tea bags. Still, it was delicious.

"I can't really believe I'm here," I said, as I poured a second cup. The five cats had joined Guennola on my bed and were watching the milk jug.

"But you are," she said, peering at me rather engagingly. Her dark hair was too long and fell into her eyes. "And it is so nice. And, after breakfast, we will sit in the garden and read an English story, and then I will show you the château and the village. There is not much to do on Mont Saint-Hilaire, but you will help me with my collection of shells, please. And you will tell me all about England. Sara told me also, but your England perhaps is different."

"I live at Hampstead, not Ealing," I told her, rather absently. In the morning light, everything seemed so sane and—no, not ordinary. For I was in the Château of Saint-Hilaire, companion to the Comte's little grandchild. But I told myself what a fool I'd been to think of mystery or anything sinister. Sara had worn silly heels and had fallen down some old stone stairs. The Comte's brother had gone.

I was going to enjoy myself and bring a little happiness into Guennola's life. Of course we'd read English books, and look for shells, and I'd talk about England all she wished. But, some time, I must get away by myself and think about how I was going to get rid of Anatole. Paris still seemed far away and in another life, but Anatole had a strange way of popping up in my mind. His earnest, rather beseeching eyes. . . . Oh, forget Anatole!

Guennola was eying my little transistor radio rather wistfully. I had put it on the table by my bed when I unpacked, but had not thought to use it. It was so tiny that I always carried it with me, but I never was one of those teen-agers who can't live without music.

Now I turned it on and she looked very pleased.

"So tiny! Me, I would love one of those. Here we have only one very big, old radio and sometimes it doesn't work."

But the music soon gave place to the news, which was the usual kind of thing . . . war . . . a Paris store broken into in the night . . . the capture of some men who had staged a holdup near Marseilles. . . missing gold.

"Nothing but crime!" I said lightly and turned it off.

After breakfast—just rolls and coffee in the French fashion—we sat in shabby deck chairs in the garden and read a book that had come from Wade's. It was quite exciting and I was nearly as absorbed in it as Guennola. I was quite surprised to find that it was eleven o'clock and that Kérity had arrived with milk and delicious homemade cakes for both of us.

"And now," said Guennola eagerly, when we had finished the last crumb, "you would like to see the château? We live in only a corner of it."

Well, I had gathered that. It was an enormous place.

She showed me a great drawing room, the furniture covered with sheets; ghostly bedrooms; vast storerooms in the kitchen regions that had once housed the food for a great rich household. The old kitchens were still in use, but at some time an attempt at modernization had been made. Kérity and the young girl were cooking at an electric stove and the prized refrigerator was humming gently. But there was still a medieval feeling to the place.

Then Guennola took me back along a dark passage to where there was a stone arch that looked very ancient and a flight of steps going down into blackness.

"This way is to the cellars—very exciting places, like caves or dungeons. All under the rock they go. But I must not take you. *Mon grandpère* has forbidden it. He says he has discovered that in some places they are not safe."

I went cautiously down two steps, peering into the darkness. The air was cold and a little musty. The thought of all that lay within the rock made my flesh creep a little and I was glad we couldn't go. Long, long ago perhaps men had been imprisoned in those cellars and perhaps, later, monks had stored their wine there. I was conscious of the weight of history.

It was an immense shock when a voice cried out in protest somewhere behind us. I thought it was Monsieur le Comte. I spun around, missed my footing on the old step, and felt myself falling.

I didn't fall far, for there was a thin iron rail and I managed to grasp it. But I was dazed and startled, looking up into Guennola's anxious face and the face of an old man she called Guildas. One of them had switched on a bare electric bulb, but it didn't do much to dispel the eerie feeling of what might have happened had I continued to fall.

"You are hurt?" Guennola gasped. She looked very white.

"No. No, I'm all right," I assured her, and we all went back to the passage above. The old man was storming at the child in the Breton language, and I recognized something of what he was saying, even in my dazed state. It was rather exciting, like finding one could see through thick glass.

He was telling her that she was very wrong to disobey Monsieur le Comte. That the place was not safe . . . that men were coming to inspect it and perhaps shore up the crumbling stone. He was so old that his eyes watered and his hands trembled as he talked.

Guennola said earnestly that we were not intending to disobey; that I had just meant to look down. Finally he went off muttering, wiping his hands on his apron.

"So much fuss," she said, quite lightly. "If you are not hurt that is all right. For a moment I thought it was like Sara and you would go away. He says that men are coming to inspect the cellars. *Grandpère* told him this morning that they are expected any day. Come, we will go out again. There is still much to see."

At the back of the château there was a long, long flight

of stone steps curving among the rocks. Down, down they went to a tiny private harbor on the sea side of the island. We descended them until we were close to the gently washing waves.

"They are never used now," explained Guennola, sitting on the bottom step. "This was the old way to the château."

From there we looked straight across the blue water. The little harbor looked deep, but was very calm.

"Can you swim?" I asked abruptly.

"But, yes. My father taught me."

"Then can't we go in? Not from here, perhaps, but from the other side." I peered over the rocks to where I could see the expanse of sand.

"If you wish," said Guennola politely, but her face had a lost, closed look.

"Didn't you swim with Sara?" I asked bluntly.

"Sometimes, yes, though Sara was not a good swimmer. Mostly she just liked to sit in the water. I did not enjoy it. Now I'm afraid of the sea."

"Well, *I'd* like to swim," I said.

We went back to the château and changed into swimsuits, then we went down the main steps toward the village. Just before we reached it, we took a side path that cut downward over the rocks to the silver-white sand. There was a blue-green pool, just deep enough to swim in, and Guennola came in with me. She could swim well and confidently, and I thought I had been right to take her swimming, though I knew she was only doing it to please me.

In the afternoon I had an interview with Madame la Comtesse. She was again by the window in her sitting room and looked anything but well. She was very charming to me, saying how grateful she was that I had agreed to stay and amuse Guennola. She even mentioned money, which had not been spoken of by either of us the previous day, promising that I would be adequately paid when I left. But, all the time she talked, I had the feeling that her thoughts were far away and very troubled.

"May we go to the mainland?" I asked. "We could look for wild flowers and I'd like to see the standing stones properly. I just glimpsed them from the bus. I never really saw Port Guenil, either."

"If you wish, my dear," she said. "I know you will look after Guennola. She understands the tides and is happier to walk across the sand these days. But if you get cut off in Port Guenil someone will bring you over. There are usually boats. Otherwise telephone. Guennola knows. She has lived here all her life."

But that day we stayed on Mont Saint-Hilaire, for, by then, the island was ringed by blue water. Guennola showed me the village. There were perhaps twenty occupied cottages and some empty ones. She introduced me to a number of people. Old women and very old men, too ancient to go out in the boats. There were two babies and some other young children, too young to go to school. She explained that when their children reached school age the people now tended to go away.

I could tell that everyone liked her, and regarded her also as the future owner. This was an atmosphere that I had never expected to find in the modern age. She was the child from the château and the château was the crux of their lives. Guennola was almost comically gracious, which went oddly with her old dress and broken sandals. I found it touching and unlikely, and it added to the feeling of being in a fairy tale. But I reminded myself that—the way things seemed now—she would never inherit Mont Saint-Hilaire and perhaps, in her secret heart, didn't wish to do so. It was not the place for anyone afraid of the sea.

She spoke mainly in the Breton language and then translated into French for me. I have no idea now why I didn't tell her that, in a strange way, I could understand. Perhaps because I wasn't prepared to try my Welsh, which was so rusty. And the half-understanding had an eerie quality, secret and fascinating. I enjoyed the feeling of having a foot in another world.

During that long, peaceful dreamlike day I saw the Comte only in the distance. Once, while exploring the château, we saw him through an open door, sitting in a kind of office, writing at a desk. Once or twice he passed through the garden when we were there and he waved to Guennola, but ignored me, or so I assumed. And when we were in the village he passed down the street toward the harbor. He nodded graciously as he went, appearing in command of his world. But his shoulders were bent and, though I did not know his age, I had the feeling that he should not look so old.

Anyway, the day passed, and, with its passing, I found I liked Guennola more and more. She was plain, she was badly dressed (she said her school clothes had been bought in Paris, but now Kérity made her summer dresses), but she had an indefinable charm. She was also sad and lonely. It seemed no life for a child, though perhaps it would have been for a happy child with loving parents. Yet, if they had lived, she would have been away at school, enjoying herself with other girls.

The sun shone until evening. The water was as blue as the sky. The château was dark, certainly, but I could not believe that it was sinister. I was convinced that Sara had been using her imagination.

In the evening, before Guennola went to bed, we sat and read in the old schoolroom that overlooked the steps that led down to the unused harbor—the sea gate, Guennola called it, for access was by a gate in the ramparts. When she had gone to bed I went back there to pack up two books for Wade's library, so that we might soon have new ones. Wade's British Bookshop—how far away it seemed!

On my way to bed I blessed the strange chance that had brought me to the Château of Saint-Hilaire. The two weeks stretched out before me like an unexpected gift that is not offered to many girls. Mary Smithson was foolish, I thought, to have turned it down.

The next morning, quite early, Guennola and I walked across the great sweep of sands to Port Guenil, with me carrying the parcel of books. Guennola was in good spirits and often ran ahead, then waited for me, smiling at me through her gently blowing hair.

We soon reached the beach that was called, she said, Plage Port Guenil, and walked the few hundred yards into the village. The post office was tiny and sleepy, in keeping with the whole place. While I was there I sent a long telegram to Céleste.

We had brought bread and cheese and some of Kérity's cakes with us, having explained that we might have a pic-nic by the standing stones but, when we left the post office, there was a bus waiting by the harbor. And, on the spur of the moment, I said:

"Would you like to go to Quimperlé?"

Guennola looked eager, but said she had no money. I

had plenty of money, and I had suddenly remembered Sara.

I made sure that there was a bus back in the afternoon and we took our seats among the women with market baskets. Guennola looked as pleased as though we were going on a long exciting excursion.

This time the narrow lanes seemed familiar and we rushed into Quimperlé before I expected it. The town looked gay in the sun and we spent a good deal of time looking at the shops and the market stalls. Then we had lunch by the river, but I had not forgotten Sara. The Comte would never know; I would warn Guennola not to mention it although I felt guilty at leading the child into deception.

"I'm going to the hospital," I said, when we had eaten all our food. "I'll ask about Sara and see if they'll let us visit her."

Guennola looked delighted.

"Now we are here I am sure *mon grandpère* wouldn't mind."

I would leave the warning until later. Why should he mind, anyway, if the nurses agreed it was all right?

"You must wait outside and, if it's all right, I'll come and fetch you. But I'll see Sara first. Be patient." Because I *had* to talk to Sara alone.

Suddenly, as we approached the building, I remembered the mystery—Sara's extraordinary letter. I didn't like the thoughts it produced, because I wanted to be happy on Mont Saint-Hilaire. But curiosity was driving me on.

The hospital was run by nuns, and the Sister in charge, somewhat to my surprise, looked pleased when she heard my request.

"But yes, mademoiselle. Sara will be delighted to have a visitor. It is Room 17. Up the stairs, there."

So I climbed the polished stairs alone and walked along a quiet corridor until I reached the room marked "17." And there I stopped, suddenly aware of all that my visit implied. Because of Sara I was in Brittany, and yet she had never heard of me.

After several moments, I knocked on the door and a young voice answered: *"Entrez, s'il vous plaît!"*

I entered and saw a small room with an empty bed. In a chair by the window sat a girl of about eighteen, with her leg stretched out on a stool. The leg was heavily encased in plaster.

My first impression was that she was unattractive. She had untidy mousy hair and a pale, slightly querulous face. She looked astonished to see me and no wonder.

"You don't know me," I said, in English. "My name is Gwenda Maitland, and I've taken your place on Mont Saint-Hilaire."

Her pale blue eyes flew wide open and she stared at me with awakening interest.

"You mean—they got another girl?"

"Mary Smithson," I said rapidly. "Only she didn't turn up. I'm there by accident." And, knowing I must be quick because Guennola was waiting outside, I told her just how I had come to arrive at Port Guenil. She heard me through with nothing but an occasional exclamation. Then, when at last I paused for breath, she said:

"Oh, I wondered where my letter had gone. I couldn't find it anywhere. I must have put it in the book by accident. I thought one of them had found it."

"But what did you *mean?*" I asked. "And how did you come to fall down the tower stairs? You can't believe—"

She looked at me for a long moment.

"I don't *know* about the stairs. I think he meant to kill me. . . . I'm almost sure I tripped over something. Maybe a string. And he was there, you see, soon after I fell, bending over me. But Kérity came, looking for one of the cats who had had kittens, I think. I was in awful pain, but I was never so glad to hear anyone's voice. She sent him for help, so he didn't have a chance to—"

"Who?" I gasped. "Not the Comte? He looks so worried, so old, but I just can't believe—"

"Not the *Comte*," she said impatiently. "Though he must be in it somewhere. His brother, Pierre Doumenjou. I'd better tell you the whole story. Perhaps *you'll* believe me."

The Meeting on the Rocks

"Why shouldn't i believe you?" I asked, after a moment or two. "I don't understand anything, so I'll be glad to have you explain. His brother's gone. He left the day after your accident. Tell me quickly, because Guennola's outside and wants to see you."

So then she began to talk, in a rapid, strained voice.

"Dave said I was imagining it all. I wondered if we should tell the police, but he was horrified at the idea. He said they'd just laugh, especially as it concerns the most respected family in the whole area. He said—Well, when I was little I did get into trouble once or twice. There was a woman next door and I saw her burying something in her garden, and her husband had disappeared, so I told people she'd killed him. I really thought she had, but then her husband came back. Dave's my brother, did you know? He has a holiday job in Vannes. They told him and he came to see me here. He says I must go to Vannes as soon as I can walk with this thing on my leg. He's tutoring a French boy, but there's a girl as well and I can teach her English. All I want now is to get away. The Comte's been very kind. He's asked them to give me every comfort here, though I know he's hard up. But I don't feel safe. I *know* I was meant to die."

"But what *happened?*" I demanded. "Why should anyone want to kill you?"

"Well, someone knows I saw them that night and I
think it was the brother. I haven't the least idea what it
was all about, but anyway . . . one night I couldn't sleep.
There'd been a queer kind of atmosphere in the château
all day, I thought, and somehow it worried me. I'd left
the book I was reading in the schoolroom, so I went along
to get it. There should have been a waning moon, but it
was a cloudy night and everywhere was pretty dark. I
took a flashlight with me. It was eleven o'clock and the
whole place is always as silent as a tomb by about ten.
For some reason I didn't switch on the schoolroom light.
I found my book and then went to the window. It was
a still, warm night and the window was wide open. I'd
switched off the flashlight to look out and then I heard
a boat. The engine was very quiet, and by then it must
have been in the old harbor below the sea gate, but I
heard it. I knew that harbor was never used, so I waited
and then I saw people. I heard them, too, though they
were trying to be very quiet. Once one of them stumbled
and cursed."

"But if it was so dark how could you see?" I asked, in-
trigued, but vaguely troubled by her tone of voice and the
wild look in her eyes.

"Well, it wasn't *quite* dark. I know there were at least
three men and I'm sure they were carrying something into
the château. It seemed so strange, especially as there'd
been a kind of tension ever since Pierre Doumenjou arrived. I waited, all shaky, and after a while they went
down again and that time they were moving quite easily.
But when they came back it was the same as before—
they were carrying something. Then just as the last man

was disappearing my finger somehow got onto the switch of the flashlight and it came on. It was quite a strong beam and I was scared to death. I had it off in a moment, but I knew it had been seen and that someone was watching."

"But the schoolroom is high above the sea gate," I said.

"Yes, but one of the men looked up. I'm sure I saw the white blur of a face. And they really did bring something to the château. It would be an ideal place for smuggling, wouldn't it? And it does go on, you know. I was kind of frozen there. Everyone had gone and it was very quiet. Then I saw Sebastien—just for a moment. The moon came out of the clouds. I *know* it was Sebastien. Whatever it is he's in it, too, and I'm not surprised." She sounded as though she didn't like Sebastien much. "And if you take my advice you'll go back to Paris as soon as you can. It's a romantic place, Mont Saint-Hilaire. I loved it at first, and that poor little girl. But I know it isn't safe. Especially as the next day, one of the fishermen was found dead on the rocks. Apparently he'd fallen and hit his head. The police came, but they seemed to think it was just death by misadventure. He was known to be rather a drunkard. He kept a lot of liquor in his cottage. But I was sure he had seen something. Oh, maybe I'm crazy, but I was really scared. And, two days later, I fell down the tower stairs."

I sat staring at her, trying to assess her extraordinary story. Parts of it had the ring of truth, but if she really was known for making up strange tales why couldn't she have made up this one? She might really have gone to the schoolroom and heard a boat. Perhaps occasionally fishermen brought a catch to the château that way.

"You don't believe me," she said flatly. "But it's true."

"Look!" I cried, glad to escape. "I must go and fetch Guennola. We won't say anything in front of her."

"Poor little thing!" she said. "She doesn't have much of a time. Her parents dead and those old grandparents. Oh, they love her all right, but it isn't the right life. Well, fetch her. I've told you all I know. And do get out quickly. It isn't a good place."

Guennola was in the entrance hall, talking to the Sister.

"May she see Sara, please, Sister?" I asked, and permission was readily given.

Guennola mounted the stairs quickly and greeted Sara joyfully. There was, clearly, a good deal of sympathy between the two. She obviously liked Sara better than I did.

"Oh, I am so pleased to see you! Does it hurt very much? Did your brother come?"

Sara told her what she had told me about going to Vannes. Then, without warning, the door opened and the Comte of Saint-Hilaire stood there. He carried a small basket of fruit and a box of chocolates. Obviously he had been warned, for he displayed no surprise at seeing us. It was impossible to know his feelings.

"I see you are much better, mademoiselle," he said formally to Sara. "That is very good. And perhaps these small gifts will help to amuse you until you can leave to join your brother. Oh, yes, Sister explained the plan. A most excellent idea. I hardly expected to find you with visitors."

Guennola had run to his side.

"Oh, Grandpère!" she cried, when he had finished speaking. "Gwenda and I came on the bus and we had a picnic by the river. You don't mind that we came to see Sara?"

"Why should I mind, my little one?" he asked. "So long

as Sara is well enough for visitors. But now she's looking tired, so we will go. I have the car outside."

And he drove us back to Port Guenil through the narrow, winding lanes, scarcely speaking at all. I kept thinking it was fortunate he didn't know I had had that time alone with Sara. Just in case there was anything in Sara's story.

A fisherman had died mysteriously the very next day. Or that very night. That was probably true; I could find out, though not from Guennola. She hadn't mentioned it, so perhaps she didn't know. A drunkard, who had missed his footing on the sharp rocks of Mont Saint-Hilaire? Or a sober man who had seen more than he should?

It was all more than I could cope with while Guennola was chattering away.

She was less cheerful later, because we had to cross to the island by boat. The old boatman who had taken me over so forcibly two days ago was waiting for us. But the sea was calm and blue and we soon reached the island. I saw her grandfather looking at her anxiously and lovingly and once more disbelief washed over me. For this handsome, worn-faced man didn't look wicked. I couldn't imagine him murdering a fisherman or tying string across an ancient stair. But Sara had not accused *him*. . . it was his brother, Pierre, she had said. Yet nothing could go on at Mont Saint-Hilaire without the knowledge of the Comte.

I had no time to think until Guennola had gone to bed, but when she had drunk her milk and settled down it was still quite light. I went out through the main door, across the garden and down the steps, seeking a place where I could sit alone and try to get things sorted out. The best possibility seemed to be the rocks near where we had bathed, though the tide was still washing against them and there was no sand in sight.

They were high black rocks and not easy to negotiate once one had left the side path that cut away from the village. But I was soon standing looking down at the sea and across to the mainland coast. How still it was! I could hear a dog barking far away across the water and even a car on the road.

I turned once and glanced up at the château brooding above me, its bastions and towers already darkening against the brilliant sunset sky. Then, leaning against a rock, I faced, at last, my questioning thoughts. Could it be true? Could something really be going on at Mont Saint-Hilaire? Smuggling, Sara had said. But what would they smuggle? What would they hide? And why would the Comte, whom I felt instinctively was basically an upright man, agree to any such thing? Because he so badly needed money; because, in five years or less, the island might have to be sold?

It was an immense shock when a voice spoke almost directly above me. The voice only said, "Hello!" but I lost my precarious balance and, scrabbling wildly, slithered down the rocks below to end up with my feet and legs in a cold sea pool.

Dazed, I heard movement above me—a long brown hand came out and grasped mine.

"I'm sorry," a voice said in French that I recognized— Parisian French. "I didn't mean to startle you. I hope you're not hurt?"

I closed my fingers on the hand and looked up into a face I remembered—the face of the young man who had sat frowning in the red car. Sebastien Doumenjou— the distant cousin.

"No," I said. "No, only wet and it's so warm it doesn't matter." I wasn't wearing stockings, so it was only my sandals and the hem of my dress.

He laughed and hauled me up until we were both on flatter rocks where we could sit down. They were still quite hot from the recent sun. Once there I took a good look at him. He had very white teeth and a nice sun-browned skin and he looked at the same time apologetic and faintly amused.

"I didn't know you were back," I said, still a little disconcerted by our unexpected and nearly disastrous meeting.

"Just come," he explained, looking a little puzzled that I seemed to know who he was. "I left my bag on the steps and came over to make the acquaintance of Mary Smithson. But I didn't mean to startle you. Please believe me."

"I'm not Mary Smithson," I said. "She didn't come." And I told him rapidly about my unconventional arrival at the château. I explained that I knew him because I had seen him from the bus, and then I found that he was frowning in much the same way he had done on that occasion.

"You really want to stay?" he asked abruptly. "You don't find it lonely or dull?"

"No. No, I love it." I was hurt by his change of manner. "It's only for two weeks, anyway; then I shall be returning to Paris."

"But it's a pity not to see more of Brittany," he said quickly. "Concarneau . . . Douarnenez . . . the north coast. Are you sure you didn't make a mistake in deciding to stay on one small island?"

"I—I don't think so. I—I'm fond of Guennola already. It's such a romantic place, isn't it?"

"I used to think so," he said somberly, "when I was young. Now I know too much about the difficulty of up-keep."

His first ease had gone, yet he was eying me with what I couldn't help but realize was appreciation. I was thankful that I had changed for supper, made up my face, and brushed my hair.

"We'd better go," he said abruptly. "Or at least I must go and report back. They go to bed early."

So I rose also, not wanting to sit there alone, and we made our way back to the steps. He picked up his bag and we entered the château together. By then the huge hall was very dim, with only one feeble light burning over the stairs.

"Think about it," he said. "There's a lot of Brittany." And he gave me a kind of salute with his left hand and walked up the stairs ahead of me and away in the direction of the rooms occupied by the Comte and Comtesse.

I stopped at the top of the stairs, quivering with an awareness I had never known before; certainly I had never known it with Anatole. I had never quite got Sebastien out of my mind since that glimpse on the road, and now he was there. His voice, his hands, his intelligent, rather reserved face. In those moments I knew that I *had* to know him better, that it was vitally important to me. Perhaps I fell in love at first—no, second sight. People say it is impossible, but I don't believe it. I don't believe it at all.

I went to my room in a complete daze, where I un-dressed and bathed. There were a great many more unanswered questions in my mind. Had he really, seriously, wanted to persuade me to go away? And, if so, why? I was almost sure he had been attracted to me instantly, or maybe that was only because it seemed so important to me.

As I got into bed I heard Sara's voice saying: "Sebastien is in it, too."

Guennola said he had come unannounced. He was, in a way, part of the family. Would he join in some nefarious affair, or was Sara utterly wrong? She had sounded very spiteful. Perhaps there was, in fact, nothing to join *in*. I hoped not, with all my heart.

Almost asleep, I remembered the vast cellars under the château. The cellars that were said, suddenly, to be unsafe. If Sara were right, something might be hidden there, in the labyrinthine depths, and perhaps that was only an excuse to keep people out.

I decided that I would try to take a look. The thought alarmed me, but I couldn't leave the mystery where it was—nebulous and upsetting.

When I slept at last, I was thinking of Sebastien as he had first looked, when he rescued me from the pool.

In the Cellars

IN THE MORNING, when Guennola and I were reading in the garden, I asked her:

"Did Sara like Sebastien?"

There had been no sign of Sebastien that morning. I didn't know if he was still in his room or out in one of the fishing boats.

Guennola looked up, pushing back her hair with that familiar gesture.

"But, yes, Gwenda. Sara was much attracted to Sebastien. Me, I noticed it at once. Always she watched him, tried to make him take notice of her."

"And—" I pressed gently. She was eleven and had been with older people most of the time. In some ways she wasn't wholly a child.

Guennola looked sad.

"Sebastien didn't seem to like Sara. He was polite, no more. She is not pretty, perhaps, but so nice. I was very sorry."

"And Sara?"

She sighed.

"Sara, I am afraid, minded very much. Quite soon she looked as though she hated Sebastien. She said things about him—that he thought himself too clever—that he was not polite. And he was *always* most polite to her."

Too polite; not interested. Poor Sara! So perhaps she had never seen him down by the sea gate on that mysterious night. Perhaps there had never been a mysterious night at all. I felt a wave of relief, coupled with real sympathy for Sara, who was plain and lonely.

Yet, somewhere in my mind, I still had the intention of exploring the cellars. If there was nothing in them, nothing mysterious, then I could forget the whole thing and enjoy myself. Later in the day, surely, I would see Sebastien.

At that very moment he materialized. He looked fresh, quite cheerful, and remarkably handsome. My heart almost stopped beating. He came straight over to us.

"You two—reading on such a lovely day! I've asked Kérity to pack up some lunch. How about coming to Concarneau? I told Gwenda last night she should see it."

Guennola sprang up.

"But, yes. How wonderful! Gwenda can take some photographs. Oh, thank you, Sebastien!"

"Thank you, Sebastien," I echoed. The day was suddenly marvelous. I rushed upstairs to find my camera and to powder my nose. Mysteries were unimportant, unreal. We were going out with Sebastien!

It was a glorious day. We drove to Concarneau and explored the romantic walled town on the island in the harbor. I took several pictures, including two of Sebastien and Guennola on the ramparts. When it was all over, I told myself, if I never saw Sebastien again, I would at least have those. For a moment I was sad, but one couldn't be sad for long on such a heavenly, happy day.

We swam at a nearby beach and ate our lunch among

the sand dunes. Guennola was in high spirits and her little face was almost pretty. She even seemed to enjoy the swim, with Sebastien always near her. There were no clouds on his face and I felt as though I had known him for quite a long time. We talked about Paris and exchanged experiences. I was so glad that he lived there. For that meant there was the faintest possibility we might meet again.

Sebastien spoke English fairly well, it turned out, but mostly we spoke in French.

We went home in the early evening, crossing the sea by boat. Mont Saint-Hilaire looked at its most beautiful, bathed in sunlight, the centuries lying gently on its old stones.

But a devil of curiosity and doubt was still with me, I realized, when Guennola had gone to bed and I thought Sebastien had gone out in the boats. He said he might do so and we had not seen him since our return. Guennola said he always dined with her grandparents.

In my room, tired but not sleepy, I suddenly remembered Sara's story and my own intention. Settle the thing once and for all, I thought, after trying to read and failing to concentrate.

It was already dark, nearly ten o'clock. Probably everyone had gone to bed; the château was utterly silent. I always packed a flashlight and it was there beside my bed. I took it up and quietly opened my door. Nothing stirred and all the lights were out. It was eerie and I didn't like the thought of that cold ancient place, but I had to find out if there was anything down there. If I found nothing, if every cellar was open and empty, then that was the end of it.

There were many staircases. I didn't need to go down

the front flight. There was one not far from my door and down I went, down to the kitchen regions, where there was no light and no sound. In the long passage I had a momentary fright, feeling something against my legs. But it was only the ginger cat, purring.

I came to the stone arch and the steps going down. I could have found the light and switched it on, but I didn't dare. I didn't know where Kérity and Guildas slept.

The steps went down quite a long way and my light went ahead into blackness. But I could see the rough stone roof. There was a cold dank smell that was very frightening, but I had gotten this far and I meant to go on.

The stairs brought me to a door which stood open. Beyond was a great vaulted room, quite empty. But there were several doors leading off it.

I tried the first door and it was locked, which gave me a nasty jolt. Then I saw an old, faded notice that said: "Wine Cellar." It was probably safe to suppose that there was wine stored there still. Even in an impoverished family there would probably be some precious bottles left.

The second door gave with only a faint creak and I looked into a room that was, as Guennola had said, almost a cave. The roof was hewn out of the living rock. Here there were some boxes, but they all seemed to be empty. They bore the name of a Paris store and the sight was curiously comforting.

I shut the door again, turning back to the great room. I could see an arched opening ahead, but there was yet another door. That one was not locked and the space beyond was certainly empty.

So I went slowly toward the vaulted arch, holding my

light out in front of me. The silence pressed on my ear-drums. I wondered anxiously how far under the château, or even the island, the underground places went. The next room—or cave—led to another one and that one to two more, branching on either side. And still I hadn't come to the end. I began to have a dreadful fear that my light wouldn't last.

Then I heard a sound behind me, scarcely more than an echo. The echo of a footstep, perhaps. In an instant I had switched off my light and stood there listening, scarcely breathing. Suddenly I felt trapped, guilty and— yes, very, very much afraid. I must have been crazy, I thought, to venture down into the cellars.

I moved backward slowly until I felt the cold stone of a wall pressing against my back. The sound came again, definitely a footstep, and now the inky darkness was broken by a dim, advancing light.

The light came nearer, until it was only a few yards away. I could see nothing beyond it as it flickered over the stone floor, the uneven walls. In another moment it would shine on me.

And then it swept around and shone into my eyes. I shrank back, feeling the horror of the unknown. *Anyone* could be behind that beam. But it was Sebastian's voice that cried, sharp with amazement and perhaps suspicion:

"Gwenda! It's you! What are you doing down here at this hour?"

"Oh, you did scare me!" I cried, as the light left my face. I switched on my own and saw him standing there, wearing an open-necked shirt and dark trousers. "I thought you'd gone out fishing."

"I decided not to; I was tired. I was looking for something to eat," Sebastien confessed, but his voice was still not quite normal. "And I heard someone along the passage. Why, you're shivering!"

"Wouldn't you be?" I asked. "It's cold down here and I thought . . . I don't know what I thought."

He took my arm and marched me firmly back through the cellars to the steps, then along the passage to the great kitchen. There he switched on a light and we surveyed each other.

"Coffee," he said abruptly and went at once to busy himself at the stove. With his back to me he said:

"Now, what sent you down into the cellars?"

I remembered that I coudn't possibly tell him the truth. So I said, rather lamely, I'm sure:

"I couldn't go to bed. I wasn't sleepy, but I was tired of reading and listening to my radio. I felt restless, so I just thought I'd explore a little. Guennola didn't show me the cellars and—and I'm fascinated by this whole place. So much history—"

"Didn't anyone tell you they're unsafe? My uncle seems quite worried about it."

"Yes. Yes, but I forgot. They seem as solid as the Rock of Ages."

"My uncle is sure that the roof of the first cellar isn't at all safe and if you'd examined it you'd have seen that the stone is breaking away. Apart from that, you might have had an accident. Sprained an ankle. Remember what happened to Sara."

How could I forget what had happened to Sara!

"Oh," I said to myself, with a wave of desolation, "is he being honest or does he really know something?"

He made the coffee and we drank it at the kitchen table. It was wonderful and I felt better. Just to be sitting there with him in the silence of the night was a deep pleasure.

Sebastien talked quite lightly, but there was something in his eyes that still troubled me a little. He was watching me and I wasn't sure if it was with admiration or speculation. Perhaps a little of both. When we had washed our cups and put everything away he said:

"Bed for both of us now, and—take my advice—don't wander around in the dark in the future. There are all kinds of hazards in this place."

We were standing close together and I wondered for a wild moment if he was going to kiss me. But he turned away, switched off the light, and led the way upstairs.

"We don't want to wake anyone up," he said. "Good night, Gwenda."

Back in my room I was beset with puzzlement, pleasure, and pain. I didn't understand anything, least of all myself.

In the morning the Comtesse sent for Guennola, saying that she wanted the child to sit with her and sew. Sebastien really had gone out in a fishing boat this time; we had seen him leave, carrying his gear, as we went down to breakfast. He had given me only a casual salute, as though we had never drunk coffee together when the château was asleep.

I wondered whether to go swimming, but I was still not cured of my curiosity. More than ever I had to know. Guennola had not taken me up any of the towers when she showed me over the château, but she had indicated the door that led to the West Tower.

"We will not go up there," she had said. "Perhaps another time when you have your camera. I am so afraid you will fall like Sara."

I took my camera as an excuse and made my way to that door. It opened with a loud creaking sound and the stairs were dark. I found a light switch and a bare bulb showed me some very ancient and worn stairs; worn with the passing of centuries of feet. Oh, certainly Sara could have fallen if she had not worn sensible heels. But, as I climbed, I was looking for any place where a string might have been tied. There was an iron handrail but that was too high. Yet, in places, there were pieces of equally thin iron that joined it, were stapled into the steps. They didn't always lie flush with the wall. It could be done, I thought, still climbing steadily. At the other side the string might be held with glue or tape. It would be enough, perhaps, to cause a missed step and easily whipped away before anyone could investigate.

At the top there was a small, heavy door that was not locked and I emerged on a flat roof, with a waist-high parapet. The view was breathtaking. I didn't wonder that Sara had wanted to paint a picture. I took several photographs, once more enchanted with the very fact of being in such a wonderful place.

I descended slowly and carefully, holding the rail firmly, for my eyes were not used to the darkness that was scarcely dispelled by the dim electric light. Oh, it would undoubtedly have been easy to fall.

I was on the third step from the bottom when the old door in front of me gave a protesting creak. Then it opened slowly and a man stood there, a man I had not see before.

"Oh, you frightened me!" I cried, in French.

He surveyed me as he spoke in a soft voice:

"Pardon me, mademoiselle. I had no intention of alarming you. But, as I came up to the château I saw you on

the tower and I wondered if anyone had warned you that the steps are not very safe."

"Yes, I knew, but I've been very careful," I said. "I was taking some photographs." I probably spoke rather wildly, for, even before he spoke again, I knew who he was. He had a look of the Comte, though much younger and tougher.

"I gather that they have found a new young lady to amuse Guennola. I am Pierre Doumenjou, the Comte's brother."

The Newcomers

"I'M GWENDA MAITLAND," I heard myself saying. "I came by chance, and—and I like Guennola so much."

He held the door open for me and I walked past him with as much dignity and assurance as I could muster.

"A charming, unfortunate child," he said. My flesh crept a little, for the tone was insincere. I knew already that I didn't at all like Pierre Doumenjou. Oh, why had he come back?

"I must go and find my brother," he was saying, "and acquaint him with my return. You will be careful of those stairs, my dear young lady?"

"I certainly will," I said and hoped my voice hadn't been too fervent. It no longer seemed extraordinary that Sara had suspected him, given her imagination. . . . But then, if there was nothing going on at the château, Pierre Doumenjou had no need to tie strings for anyone's unwary feet.

Bewildered, not at all happy, I went to the schoolroom and found Guennola there. She told me that her grandmother had soon tired of her company. She had said she didn't feel well.

"Your uncle is back. Did you know?" I asked.

Guennola flushed.

"No. Oh, Gwenda, are you sure?"

"Yes, I talked to him. Why do you dislike him so much?"

"Never have I liked him," she said passionately. "Sometimes he tries to be kind, but I do not feel that he means it. He brings me presents; last time a doll from Paris. I lost her overboard," she added, in strange triumph.

"Oh, Guennola!"

"But I dropped her," she said innocently. "And the sea took her away. The sea will take anyone."

I nearly said, "Oh, Guennola!" again, but stopped the words just in time. I didn't like the expression on her face.

"Come out into the garden and let's read," I suggested. No books had come yet from Wade's, but there were plenty of books on the shelves, some of them in English. Most had "To Guennola from Papa and Maman" on the flyleaf.

So we read and later went down to swim in the safe pool. And there Guennola had her first tantrum, going red in the face and absolutely refusing to enter the water. I didn't insist. How could I when she was so upset? And then I saw that Pierre Doumenjou was watching us from the rocks high above.

He soon turned away and disappeared and I had a short swim alone, but didn't enjoy it. I was too aware of tension. Guennola was calm again when I returned to her. She even made an attempt at apology.

"Me, I usually like to swim with you, but he was watching us and that I *didn't* like!"

An hour later we saw her uncle in the distance, with the Comte, and I realized that the Comte looked dreadful. Very bent about the shoulders and old.

Kérity, meeting us at lunchtime, looked vexed.

"Another one to cook for, and him I do not like! So different from Monsieur le Comte. He brings trouble with him."

"Trouble?" I echoed, and the old woman tossed her head.

"I do not know what kind of trouble, but always Monsieur looks worse when he is here, and he is a sick man."

Perhaps he was; he had looked terrible.

In the afternoon Guennola and I searched for shells and then spent an hour or two drawing. She drew much better than I did. Her pictures of the island had a strange clarity, childish but true.

The day seemed unusually long and I found it a real effort to amuse her. I missed Sebastien and was made uneasy by my own thoughts. My lovely enchanted island seemed to have quite a different atmosphere. I told myself that it was nonsense to feel everything had changed just because the Comte's brother had come, but when I saw the Comtesse briefly before supper I was shocked to see how upset she was. She spoke to me charmingly, however, and explained that her leg was troubling her.

Guennola and I were just sitting down to supper when —miracle of miracles—Sebastien came in, tall, even more suntanned than usual, and still in the clothes in which he had gone fishing.

"I'm going to eat with you," he announced. My first impression that he looked frowning and strange was quickly dispelled, because he was soon joking with Guennola. But at the end of the meal, he said:

"My uncle and aunt have company enough."

"Don't you like him, either?" Guennola asked, with her head on one side, and he flicked her under the chin.

"Let's say I prefer other company, little one. Besides, I wasn't prepared to change my clothes. I knew you'd both forgive me."

He left us then, and soon I took Guennola up to bed. I was glad that the day was almost over, but could not quite have said why. I tried to remind myself that I ought to treasure each day, because time was passing and soon Mont Saint-Hilaire would be only a memory.

The next day Guennola seemed in better spirits and soon everything had changed for me. She and I were down by the harbor when the launch came in. The boat was laden well past the gunwales with great pieces of wood and there were three strange men on board—elderly men in working clothes.

"So they have come to mend the cellar roof!" Guennola cried excitedly.

"Really?" I asked, in utter astonishment. I could hardly believe it.

"But, yes. *Mon grandpère* told me this morning. They are to live in one of the empty cottages, where food has been provided. Stonemasons from Brest."

The old boatman who had brought me over on that first day was edging the boat carefully toward the steps. They had only just got over before the tide went out.

I looked down at the strangers. Stonemasons from Brest! Oh, if that were true then there really couldn't be anything hidden in the cellars. The whole thing was a figment of Sara's imagination and mine. The three looked tough, but quite ordinary.

We stayed and watched as the stuff was unloaded, not without difficulty, as the water was getting lower every moment and the steps were slippery. There was a lot of wood, very thick and strong, then crates, one of them very heavy. Finally there were three suitcases that presumably held the men's personal possessions.

There was a lot of shouting and gesticulating. Soon all four men were very hot, their foreheads glistening with sweat. Then suddenly Pierre Doumenjou was there, saying in French—though all three strangers had been speaking in Breton:

"My brother, the Comte, asked me to greet you. All this stuff will have to be taken up to the château. I've asked several of the fishermen to help. But first I'll take you to where you are to live."

The men thanked him, took up their suitcases, and followed him away to the gap between the cottages.

My relief was so enormous that I could have danced and sung. Nothing, nothing could be hidden in the cellars when they were admitting three total strangers to work there. The whole thing had definitely been nonsense—a figment of poor Sara's nervous, unsatisfied mind. And I was nearly as silly, because I had almost believed her.

Pierre Doumenjou was still on the island, of course, but we didn't need to see much of him. In fact, we'd go away from the island for the rest of the day. It was twelve o'clock, so we'd take our lunch and perhaps have a picnic by the standing stones.

Kérity didn't seem to mind and had soon packed us up some cold meat, crusty bread, and some of her delicious cakes. We sat among the stones and ate the good food, and I still found *Les Jeunes Filles* a little eerie because of their very ancientness, but the sky was so blue and the sun so hot that the story seemed just a story. They had never been young girls, that was quite certain! They must have had some strange purpose in times long past and unrecorded.

When we returned to the château Guennola went quite naturally toward the entrance to the cellars and I followed. Some of the wood was in place, supporting the roof, and, though it was six o'clock, we could see (and hear) one of the men still at work.

Sebastien found us there. I didn't know of his presence until he spoke above the sound of banging.

"So, it'll soon be safe. Did you have a good day, the two of you?"

"But, yes, it was lovely!" Guennola told him, as we retreated up the steps.

I wasn't sure that Sebastien had enjoyed his day, whatever he had been doing, for his face looked dark and frowning. Yet perhaps that was a wrong impression, as it had seemed so often before, for, when we reached full daylight, he was smiling.

"Shall I see you tonight, Gwenda?" he asked. "When Guennola has gone to bed?"

"Aren't you having your supper with us?" Guennola demanded.

"Alas, no, my child. I'm summoned to dinner with the others."

Guennola looked from him to me. I hastily composed my face, because Guennola was very observant and I didn't want my feelings to show. She had guessed Sara's and she wasn't going to guess about mine, nor was Sebastien—not yet. It was enough that he was there and I was going to see him later.

"On the steps, outside the gate in the ramparts," he said to me, before he hurried away.

"I am so glad that Sebastien likes you," Guennola said happily.

I waited where he had said when Guennola had gone to bed. After the lovely day the sky was very clear, flushed with color. I leaned on the old wall and looked down at the cottages. It was very peaceful, very still. I could hear voices far away by the harbor. Nearer, almost below me, was one of the hitherto empty cottages. Now smoke curled from the chimney and the three men from Brest were sitting on a bench outside the door, drinking something— probably coffee—out of big cups. They were in their shirt sleeves and looked relaxed. Two were smoking and one was reading a crumpled newspaper.

I stared down at them, glad that no one had known about my wild suspicious thoughts. Yet if it had not been for the suggestion of mystery I would not have been there at all, and that, somehow, was unthinkable. I couldn't imagine now never having gotten to know Mont Saint-Hilaire. They were so real and important; Guennola and her grandfather and grandmother. Sebastien—No, I could not quite face how important Sebastien already was to me.

Leaning there, I groped in my handbag, which I always carried with me, and took out Sara's letter. Now I could look at it kindly, understanding better how she had come to write it. Poor Sara, with her loneliness and her flowering imagination. I really must burn the letter when I got a chance. There was no point at all in keeping it.

I had scarcely put it away when there was a footfall above me and Sebastien appeared.

"There you are, Gwenda! And what a beautiful evening! Shall we walk by the harbor?"

We strolled right out to the end of the breakwater. It was so quiet and windless, so beautiful. Sebastien talked about Paris and then about Guennola.

"Poor child," he said, "it isn't the right life now that her parents have gone."

"But what other life could she have?" I asked. "The only alternative seems to be a return to boarding school."

"Even that would be better. Probably they'll send her in the autumn. She isn't really happy on Mont Saint-Hilaire any more. She'd be better away forever, in a new environment."

"But she belongs here. She'll own it, won't she?" I asked.

Now he certainly was frowning. His dark brows almost met.

"There's not much money. You know that? She'll only inherit a problem, if the island is still in the family then. Soon I will be going back to Paris, and, in a short while, you'll go too. I've suggested that she stay with my parents for a time. Mother would be glad to have her."

"Oh!" I said. "Perhaps that would be a good idea." And my heart was light, because it would seem natural for me to visit Guennola. I would genuinely *want* to see her.

It was almost dark when we climbed the steps again. Silence had fallen between us and I was startled when Sebastien said, in quite a different voice from the one he had used so far:

"I still think you should see more of Brittany before your holiday is over."

"I can—another time," I offered, shaken.

"But why not give yourself a few days now? I'll try and persuade them to let me take Guennola away soon. The Comte would agree, but my aunt clings to the child, even though she doesn't see much of her."

I didn't answer. I couldn't understand the sense of urgency. The arrival of the stonemasons had proved that there was no mystery. I had thought that I could spend the rest of my time on Mont Saint-Hilaire in peace. And now here was Sebastien still trying to persuade me to go away.

We were under the shadow of the great gate. Sebastien suddenly drew me to him and kissed me. It was so unexpected, and so wonderful, that I was stunned for a moment. Then I responded.

We stayed there, close together for a few moments, and I knew without doubt that I was happier than I had ever been in my life. Then he drew away, took my hand, and pushed open the little door in the big one.

He never said another word as we walked into the château and across the shadowy hall. Then he released me and said, "Good night!" and walked away up the stairs.

I sat down on the bottom stair, to savor my strange joy. I wondered if he really liked me. If that sudden, quite unexpected kiss had meant anything more than that it was a lovely evening and he thought me pretty.

In bed, some time later, I was still drowned in the enchantment, but also I couldn't help puzzling over his evident desire to get me—and Guennola—away from Mont Saint-Hilaire.

There was nothing hidden—there couldn't be. Sebastien was just on holiday and not involved in anything. Yet, somewhere deep in my mind, there was still a dark questioning corner.

Shocks for Gwenda

BY THE NEXT DAY, however, my vague suspicions were more or less lulled again, and I could only remember Sebastien's kiss. The sun was still shining warmly and Guennola was in good enough spirits. Her uncle was still on the island, but we saw little of him. I was careful to keep her out of the way.

That morning a card came from Sara to Guennola, saying that she was now in Vannes. She had to visit the hospital there, but she was enjoying living with the French family and teaching the little girl English. So that seemed to take care of Sara, though the result of her mysterious letter still remained, in as much as I was there at Mont Saint-Hilaire.

The sound of banging echoed up from the cellars, so the work really seemed to be getting done. I told myself that there was not the least need to worry any more, yet it made me uneasy to see the Comte, for he looked no better. If anything he looked much worse.

Guennola, too, noticed this and was concerned.

"Oh, I know *Grandpère* is not well!" she cried, when we had seen him in the village street. "And *Grandmère* is worried about him; I know she is. They are both getting so *old.*"

Poor child, she had only those two left to her now, and, though I had been feeling so much happier, I felt a momentary surge of anxiety.

I had decided to take Guennola to Quimperlé again and we agreed to do some shopping for Kérity, who said she was too old to go traipsing that far. In fact, she rarely even went to Port Guenil. Most of the food and other necessities were ordered by telephone or letter and sent across to Mont Saint-Hilaire.

As well as going to Quimperlé we also spent some time in Port Guenil, where they were getting ready for the *pardon,* or blessing of the fishing boats and nets. It was easy to see that the village would be festive, for flags and bunting were going up and they were also draping the blue nets used in the sardine fishing from house to house in the narrower streets, so that one walked under shifting shadows.

Guennola was quite excited by this and when we got home she showed me the lovely Breton costume she would wear. It had been in the family for several generations and was rich with velvet and lace. Though I hardly thought she could have grown much, it was just a little too small for her, so I sat down to let out a few of the seams, working carefully on the beautiful material. She also found a costume for me, which she insisted I wear.

Except for a few minutes in the morning, we hadn't seen Sebastien all day, but we met him as we were walking along the corridor to my room. I had the two dresses over my arm and was talking to Guennola, when suddenly I became aware of his presence. The corridor was always dark, but I realized that he looked rather strange. And he had a big bandage on his face.

"What's the matter?" I asked sharply. "What's happened?"

"I had an accident in the car," he said, then, with a glance at Guennola, "No need to worry. It might have been much worse. Kérity told me you'd gone to Quimperlé and I was going to find you and help to bring back the shopping. But I was scarcely out of Port Guenil when something went wrong with the steering. If anything had been coming the other way it wouldn't have been so good, but as it was I just came in rather violent contact with the high bank on my left."

"Oh, dear!" I gasped. "And you cut your face."

"It's nothing much; the doctor fixed it. But the car's out of action for a few days. I had it towed to the garage."

"Oh, Sebastien, how dreadful!" wailed Guennola, and he patted her shoulder.

"I'm still here to tell the tale, little one." But these light words were belied by his expression and his general air of tenseness.

I knew he loved that old car dearly and put the fact that he was so upset down to that.

When Guennola had gone to bed I tried to find him, but he was nowhere around. And at least there was probably one good thing about the accident; he would no doubt stay until the car was mended. Much as I loved Mont Saint-Hilaire, I knew it wouldn't be the same without the chance of seeing Sebastien.

When Guennola and I were in Port Guenil the next day Sebastien suddenly strode up to us. He might have been a fisherman he was so suntanned and wearing such old clothes, and the bandage on his face added to his disreputable appearance. But I loved him that way and could hardly imagine what he must look like in Paris.

"Come and have some fruit drinks," he suggested.

Guennola enjoyed her drink, but presently wandered away to talk to some old women by the cottages. Sebastien and I stayed there at the little outdoor table. I would have liked to hear more about his accident, but he didn't give me a chance.

In his lighter moods he was certainly a good talker and he spoke of places he had visited. His real love was Switzerland, where he had done a lot of climbing, and he said he might go to Kandersteg in the autumn. He had intended to go during the summer, but his friend couldn't make it and so he had come to Mont Saint-Hilaire instead.

I had done a little climbing, too, in Wales and once in the Cuillin of Skye, with some older friends who were quite experienced. It was a joy to find we had a good many things in common—a love of books, music and the theater, as well as climbing and exploring new country.

While we sat there in the sun I was so happy—so completely content. I had known him for just a short time, and some of that time had been spoiled by vague suspicion and fear, but now, I told myself, all was well. He liked me—I was sure he liked me.

Guennola came running back and Sebastien rose to his feet.

"Well, I must go and see how they're getting on with the car," he said.

Guennola wanted to go with him; but he said no, he didn't want us to see the car in its sad state. So we said good-bye and set off to walk across the shore. And then I got a nasty shock, for suddenly Guennola said:

"I told *Grandpère* that of course I wouldn't go away to Paris. Not until you go, Gwenda. Then you can take me with you and I will stay with Sebastien's mother. Perhaps Sebastien will take us both in his car, for it will be mended by then."

"I didn't know your grandfather had mentioned it," I said, looking at her searchingly. I was surprised that she had kept it to herself all day.

"But, yes. He called me into the office after breakfast, when you were finishing your letter to Céleste. He said Sebastien could borrow his car and drive me there. But he only *asked* me and I said no, thank you. Because of course I won't go before the *pardon*."

I looked around me at the great sweep of sand, at the island rising in all its beauty against the summer sky. If the Comte insisted, then that meant my days on Mont Saint-Hilaire were even more numbered than I had thought. But why *should* he insist? There couldn't be any urgency. Guennola was very happy with me. She had even gotten out some of her lesson books and said perhaps we would do some work when the *pardon* was over.

I knew then what a great spell the island and Brittany itself had cast over me. It had not always been a happy spell—not in those first days. But oh, I loved that place so! In my mind Brittany had somehow fused with that other country I had adored as a child and loved still: Wales. The seascapes here were very like those near my grandmother's house. It was something in the air as well as in the ancient earth.

Even the people had a similar look. And then there was the language. Over the language I still hugged my secret knowledge. Once or twice I had nearly explained to Guennola, but, strangely, something had always stopped me. Later, and not so much later, either, I was to be thankful that some unexpected secrecy in myself had made me remain silent. For Guennola would almost certainly have told others, and, if that had happened, she might not have remained safe.

But I had no knowledge of any danger to her as she ran and leaped over the sand, sometimes stopping to do a wild little dance. She was a graceful child and I had stopped thinking she was plain. With her bare brown limbs and flying dark hair she looked quite different from the child who had first appeared through the gate in the ramparts. And behind her, as she danced, was the island that was her home, her inheritance. It was a picture of romance and tragedy all rolled into one.

Then she stopped dancing and suddenly drooped, in the way she had. She hadn't really much energy and she was certainly far too thin and small.

"Sometimes I am happy and then I remember. . . . It's so beautiful now, but in winter it will frighten me. The sea—I don't like the wild sea!"

How could she, when it had taken her father and mother? And then I thought that perhaps she would be better off in a Paris flat.

When we returned we swam in the pool, as we did most days, either morning or evening. Then we went to our rooms to get clean and tidy for supper. In fact, I always changed my dress and took special care with my appearance. Perhaps I would have done it, anyway, but I always hoped that there might be a walk with Sebastien, if he was not out in the boats or helping the fishermen with work on the nets. He even helped to paint boats sometimes. He seemed to be handy at most things and was on friendly terms with everyone on the island.

When I was ready I stared at myself in the glass. I was very much suntanned and my hair was bleached by the sun until it shone with a silvery gleam. My lime-green dress suited me and I was glad that I had packed it, along with a blue one and a yellow one. They were all very thin and drip-dry, so really I had enough to wear with the tan one in which I had traveled.

I couldn't find my favorite lipstick and thought probably I had dropped it into my handbag. That handbag was quite a joke with Guennola and Sebastien, because it was big and I kept so many things in it—most of my make-up, suntan cream, sunglasses, scissors, sewing materials.

I was rooting through it, pushing aside a card from Céleste and a few other papers, when I remembered that I still had Sara's letter, and that was silly. It was really stupid of me to keep it. There was a pocket with a zipper in the middle and I kept most of my money there, with my return railway ticket. And I had always put the letter there for safekeeping.

It wasn't there now! Unbelieving at first, I searched through the whole bag again, then turned out the entire contents on the bed. The letter certainly wasn't there.

Slowly I put everything back, then sat down on the bed with a bump, utterly puzzled and dismayed. I couldn't have dropped it by accident; not when it was always safely behind the zipper. Of course I took out money occasionally, but I was sure I couldn't have dislodged the letter. The only possible explanation was that someone had taken it.

It couldn't really matter. I had proven to myself that the mystery had only been Sara's imagination. But who could have taken it? I was sure that Guennola would never open my bag. She was an honest child, and not inquisitive.

The answer seemed to be that anyone could have taken it. I often left the bag on the rocks while we swam, and once, while we were looking for shells (the previous day,

hadn't it been, before we went to Quimperlé?), I had actually forgotten it. It was still there when we went back.
Everyone on Mont Saint-Hilaire was honest, Guennola
had said.

She arrived then, telling me that supper was ready,
and she looked at me anxiously.

"What is it, Gwenda? Oh, you look so pretty!"

"Nothing," I answered. "Nothing. I'm hungry, aren't
you?"

I tried to talk as usual during the meal, but I was still
puzzled and upset. Who had we seen while we were
looking for shells? Well, Sebastien . . . He had been on
his way to the harbor, but had come out of his way over
the rocks for a chat. And Pierre Doumenjou had been on
the rocks above us as we returned to look for the bag. Anyone else could have been there, because, for some of the
time, we had been out of sight in a sandy dip among the
rocks, quite a distance away.

Sebastien. . . Pierre Doumenjou. No, not Sebastien, I
told myself. *He* wouldn't look in my bag. And why should
the Comte's brother do so? I had scarcely spoken to him
since that first encounter. And, if there were no mystery,
he had no cause to feel any interest in me or my possessions.

I was dreadfully uneasy, all the same, for I didn't like
to think of that letter in uncomprehending hands. Oh,
what a *fool* I'd been to keep it! What a fool I'd been not
to notice earlier that it had disappeared. Just when Guennola was in bed Kérity came to me with a message. Monsieur le Comte wished to see me in his office.

My heart leaped. He had taken so little notice of me;
what could he want?

I went downstairs very slowly and found the office door

open. The Comte was writing at his desk, and I observed again how his shoulders drooped. He rose when he heard me and greeted me courteously, shutting the door and indicating a chair.

"Mademoiselle," he said formally, "you have been very kind to stay here and amuse Guennola. My wife and I are deeply grateful for the trouble you have taken to keep her happy, and she likes you, we both know."

Well, that was handsome of him. I had been sure, at first, that he didn't want me to stay. But what was he leading up to? I found that I was tense with anxiety—with awareness. Already I knew what was coming.

Danger

He was continuing slowly:

"I asked Guennola this morning, and it is true that she is not very keen to go to Paris immediately. But we both feel that we've trespassed on your time for long enough. You still have a few days' holiday left and it's only fair that you should have a chance to see more of our beautiful Brittany. Tomorrow is the *pardon,* but on the next morning Guennola is to travel to Paris to stay with Sebastien's father and mother. They are charming people and Madame Doumenjou loves children. She'll give Guennola a good time and we feel she should have a change of scene. This is not a happy place for her now."

"Yes, monsieur, I quite understand," I said quietly. So it was nearly over, the strange time on Mont Saint-Hilaire! "And—and will Sebastien drive her to Paris?"

He frowned.

"That was my first idea. He could have borrowed my car. But Sebastien says he thinks it is too far for her. She's a restless, nervous child in many ways and in a train she will not have to sit so still. As it happens the wife of one of the fishermen is going to Paris. She makes the journey fairly often as she has a daughter living there. The daugh-

ter married quite well and sends her the fare. So either
Sebastien or I will drive them to Quimperlé." He gave
me a long look from his deep-set eyes. "Thank you, Mademoiselle Gwenda. I owe you much. In some small recom-
pense perhaps you will accept this." He handed me some
bills. "And I hope you will enjoy the rest of your stay in
Brittany. You will, of course, remain for the *pardon;*
Guennola will wish your company. Maybe you would
like a lift to Quimperlé when she leaves?"

"Thank you. Yes. But there's no need for *this,"* I
gasped. "I've loved it here. I love Guennola. Oh, please—"

"Keep it, mademoiselle," he said. "You have more than
earned it. Perhaps you'll visit Guennola in Paris?"

I got myself out somehow, still clutching the money
that I didn't want. I was surprised at the sick misery that
filled me. I told myself that it had to end, and it was only
doing so a few days earlier than I had expected. I told
myself that if Sebastien wished it, we could meet again
in Paris.

I found myself out in the great hall, where the front
door was still open. And standing in the doorway was
Sebastien. He came to me quickly and took my arm.

"What's the matter?" he asked.

I struggled for composure.

"Nothing, really. I—I've just heard that Guennola's
going to Paris the day after tomorrow."

"I know," he said. "My mother wants her. She'll take
her up the Eiffel Tower and on a *bateau mouche.* Ever
since we all grew up my mother has been deprived. And
she loves Guennola."

"So it's over," I said.

The hall was dim. Not even the one bulb was lighted.
He suddenly took my face in his hands.

"Have you liked it so much? It's not a very cheerful household."

"Then why do you stay?" I found myself asking. "Why didn't you drive Guennola to Paris, as the Comte wanted?"

I couldn't see his face. He said, after a moment:

"I felt compelled to stay a short while longer." Then he kissed me, adding, when we were a little apart, "We both live in Paris, remember. We may easily meet again."

And then Pierre Doumenjou came through the hall. His presence effectively broke the spell. Sebastien turned away toward the door and I went quickly up the stairs.

I was dead tired suddenly. I should have been happy, because Sebastien seemed to mean us to meet again, but somehow I wasn't. The tensions were all back again, though I couldn't really understand why.

Guennola took the news well about going to Paris. She was already wearing her Breton costume when her grandfather sent for her, and perhaps the fact that she wasn't to miss the festive day helped. She came to my bedroom, where I was obediently struggling into the yards of velvet and lace.

"*Mon grandpère* wishes me to go to Paris, and *Grandmère* also says perhaps it will be a good idea. But I think Sebastien's mean not to take me."

"It is a very long way," I pointed out. "The train will probably be quicker. And then Sebastien would have to bring the car back."

"I wish you would come also."

I didn't know whether to return to Paris with her, or to try and continue my holiday. I did want to see more of Brittany, but not then. How *could* I enjoy wandering to Douarnenez or somewhere when my mind was wholly occupied with Mont Saint-Hilaire and the people at the château? I had a strange feeling that there was no life ahead; as though it stopped the very next day. And that was silly.

"I'll see," I said, after a moment.

"But you have still some days of your holiday. It is selfish of me," Guennola said contritely.

"Help me to do up this bodice."

When I was dressed I hardly knew myself. The full velvet skirt fell past my calves, the bodice shaped my figure and the white lace around my shoulders suited me. The elaborate *coiffe* presented some difficulties, but was finally safely anchored in place.

"I have no right to it," I said. "But it's very beautiful."

"People will think you are Breton," Guennola said with delight. "Oh, come and show Sebastien!"

"Hasn't he gone out in the boats?" I asked, suddenly shy.

"The boats do not go out today. Everyone will stay. There is a procession. The priest blesses the boats. He will come across the sea—" it was going to be high tide during the morning—"and bless our boats here. We also have a little share in the *pardon*."

Well, I should have known that. There were blue nets over our one little street, too.

Sebastien met us on the stairs. He was not in his fishing clothes, but wore a clean white shirt and gray trousers. His gaze flew to my attire in astonishment.

"Gwenda! I hardly knew you. How splendid you look!"

"I'm a Breton lass for a few hours." I tried to speak lightly, but I was conscious of his continued stare. "Guennola insisted."

"But, Sebastien, you should wear a Breton costume also!"

Guennola protested. "Come, I will find you one. You are a Doumenjou, even if you do live in Paris."

He pulled her hair and nearly knocked off the carefully arranged *coiffe*. To my surprise Guennola at once became fretful.

"Oh, now you've spoiled it!"

"No. No, I haven't. Don't wail, child. And make up your mind to it, I'm not going around in any Breton costume. But I'll come over with you to see the fun."

"It is not all fun," Guennola said reproachfully. "It's *religious*."

"All right. I know that, of course. I was attending the *pardon* when you were so high." And he measured a foot from the floor.

"You were not. You were always at school."

"Wrong, then. One summer I had mumps and came here to recuperate. And another time there was a different reason. I forget."

We went down the steps toward the harbor, meeting the three stonemasons on the way. They gave us polite greetings, but when they had gone I saw that Sebastien was frowning and Guennola again looked fretful.

"I don't like those men!" she announced.

"You've scarcely seen them," I remarked. Yet I wasn't sure that I liked them myself. They had bold stares and unpleasant expressions.

"Still I do not like them. They're too friendly with my uncle. Last night they were all laughing in his room."

"How do you know?" Sebastien asked sharply.

"Me, I couldn't sleep. I wanted a drink of water. So I went to the bathroom. His room is down the little stairs not far from there. They were laughing in a bad way and drinking. The door was open. They saw me and Oncle Pierre told me to go back to bed. Then he shut the door."

Sebastien frowned harder than ever and I felt dismayed and puzzled. But I had no time to pursue any thoughts because the launch was waiting and we were going to be late if we didn't hurry. We ran down the little street, under the flickering arch of nets, then down the steps and over the cobblestones of the harbor. But at the last Guennola hung back.

"But where is *Grandpère?* He has to come to Mass. Everyone will be so upset if he doesn't!"

"Perhaps he's gone already," said Sebastien. "If not, there are other boats going over. Don't worry, Guennola. He'll be there."

When we reached Port Guenil I really did almost forget Guennola's disturbing words about her uncle because it was so lovely and moving. First there was Mass in the tiny church near the harbor, with all the older people and some of the younger ones wearing their traditional costumes. There were also a great many tourists, so that the church was very crowded. I am not Catholic, yet I found it very peaceful and impressive.

Just after Mass started there was a slight stir and I turned around to see that the Comte had arrived and that he was kneeling at the back. His brother was with him and was looking arrogantly about, not praying. So they must have followed us in another boat.

Oh, I shall never forget it. . . the procession that followed, the blessing of the boats. We from the château all returned with the priest and the ceremony was repeated on Mont Saint-Hilaire. The Comte, I noticed, looked like a man in a dream, or more accurately a nightmare, but he was very gracious to everyone. Pierre Doumenjou re-

tained his air of arrogance and slight amusement, but it
was easy to see that he wasn't popular. Few people spoke
to him.

We had lunch at the château, then, as the tide had
gone out sufficiently, Guennola and I walked back to Port
Guenil. Sebastien had said that he might join us later.
By then we had abandoned our costumes; they were far
too hot. In fact, Guennola kept on complaining about being too warm, and she was rather flushed. I was a little
worried about her, but she cheered up when we reached
the village, which was very gay and crowded. There
seemed even more visitors and cars than there had been
during the morning.

There were stalls selling balloons, ice cream, and such
things as Breton dolls, and some of the older people were
dancing the ancient round dances in a cleared space. The
younger ones occasionally joined in, but ineptly. It was
clear that, even in remote Port Guenil, the old ways were
passing. The young people were more interested in "pop"
music than in folk tunes.

I took a number of pictures and bought two of the
Breton dolls for my sisters. The dolls were very pretty and
would adorn their bedrooms; both girls were too old to
play with dolls.

It was very hot, hotter than it had been so far, but the
sunshine wasn't very clear and there was a heavy, thundery feeling in the air, which increased as the afternoon
wore on.

Sebastien joined us, as we stood watching the dancing,
so of course I immediately felt happier.

"You and Gwenda should dance," said Guennola.

Sebastien and I looked at each other and laughed.

"I'm not very good at this kind of dancing," said Sebastien. "One day Gwenda and I will dance in a very different place."

Oh, yes, I should have been very happy, if things had been just a little different. But I was worried about Guennola, who seemed increasingly fretful, and, as I had seen both Pierre Doumenjou and one of the stonemasons in the crowd, I couldn't wholly forget affairs at Mont Saint-Hilaire.

Presently Sebastien mopped his brow and suggested that we should take a stroll away from the village. It was growing, he said, almost too noisy and crowded. So we walked slowly along the narrow road by the beach, where it was certainly a little cooler, then turned inland.

The scent of the gorse was very heavy in the thundery air, and there were a good many parked cars, wherever the road was wide enough, but almost no people. They were all drawn to the dancing and stalls in Port Guenil.

We came, after a short time, in sight of *Les Jeunes Filles* and Guennola suggested that we should go and sit in their shade. So we crossed the field and settled ourselves in the shadow cast by the largest stone. It was very peaceful there, though, as always, a little eerie. The wind-blown wood came, on the one side, almost up to the stones and there were great banks of gorse.

The gorse crackled and popped in the heat and there was a loud hum of insects. We sprawled on the grass and I think we all almost fell asleep. Sebastien was very near me, but he didn't touch me. I lay looking at him, wondering just when and how we would meet again. And then it occurred to me that I definitely should have to get rid of poor Anatole. I had almost forgotten him, but suddenly guilt surged up into my mind. He thought I was in London with my family and here I was lying by some ancient stones in Brittany with quite another love.

Guennola suddenly sat up and said:

"Me, I have a headache. I want to go home."

"Perhaps we'd better," I agreed, after feeling her head. She really was much too hot.

"But first you'll take a picture of Sebastien on top of a stone."

"I'm no *jeune fille!*" Sebastien teased. But he climbed up onto the highest stone and stood looking down at us.

"All right, I will," I said and picked up my camera. For, after all, it would be my last Breton picture. I had almost made up my mind to return to Paris with Guennola.

I took the picture and I was just saying, "Thank you. I've got it!" when there was a sharp crack from the wood.

At the same moment Sebastien had started to move, ready to jump down. Then he gave a startled yelp and put his hand to his ear. In another moment he was sprawling on the grass, his face very white.

Guennola had screamed; I don't think I made a sound. It all happened too quickly.

"Get down. Keep down!" Sebastien ordered.

We obeyed. I had my arm over Guennola's shoulders. She was shaking.

"But it was a shot! Oh, you might have been killed, Sebastien!" she almost sobbed.

"It certainly was," said Sebastien. "It singed my ear. If I hadn't moved. . . ." Then he seemed to realize that he must make light of it for Guennola's sake and perhaps for mine. "Someone after rabbits, no doubt."

"But they couldn't . . . Who would?" I asked. The

stones were between us and the wood and there was no other sound but the passing of a car on the road.

"Very careless of someone," said Sebastien. "And, just in case it should happen again, keep down and run for the gorse."

"But—" I began.

He gave me a quelling look. His face was grim.

"Go on. Quickly!"

I took Guennola's hand and we ducked among the gorse bushes, with Sebastien at our heels. Guennola's hand was very hot and she seemed half-paralyzed with fear.

"There's no danger now," said Sebastien, as we climbed through a gap in the bank on to the road. "Never mind, Guennola. It was just an accident."

"But shouldn't you tell the police?" I asked, as we walked quite quickly back to the beach. But, even as I

spoke, I remembered that the "police" in Port Guenil con-
sisted of one elderly man, not very bright. I had met him
with Guennola, who, of course, knew everyone.

"No," said Sebastien. "No, not now. We must get this
child home. Just someone shooting at rabbits."

But I knew, as we headed across the shore, that he
didn't believe it. Someone had intended to shoot him and
he was aware of it. Guennola was dragging behind us,
wailing that her headache was very bad. I had a headache
myself and my thoughts were racing. But, once again, I
didn't understand anything.

The Gathering Storm

I KNEW THAT SEBASTIEN was very uneasy until we were well out over the sand—still, even then he glanced behind us occasionally. But there was probably no more danger, because the road was very open at that point, with nowhere to hide, and there were a number of tourists sitting on the beach.

The atmosphere was heavier than ever and that was probably what was upsetting Guennola, though of course the fright hadn't helped.

She hung back as we climbed the steps to the gate in the ramparts, wailing that she was too tired to climb them. So Sebastien swung her up in his arms. Over her dark head his eyes met mine.

I was relieved when we met Kérity in the garden. The old woman had known Guennola all her life and had been more or less nurse to her.

Kérity felt the child's forehead and said:

"The little one has had too much sun, and it's going to thunder sooner or later. She doesn't like thunder. She had better lie down. It's always cool in her room."

I fully intended to stay with Sebastien, because I *had* to talk to him, but Guennola said urgently:

"You come, too, Gwenda, please."

"But—" I began, looking at Sebastien appealingly. He met my gaze blankly and almost imperceptibly shook his head.

"I *have* to talk to you," I said, still hanging back. "They were not shooting rabbits. Someone meant to shoot *you*. And perhaps that business with your car wasn't an accident."

"Not now," he said. "Go with Guennola. And don't use your imagination too much. By tomorrow you'll be away from Mont Saint-Hilaire."

Helpless and upset, I turned and followed Guennola and Kérity. He wasn't going to confide in me and he had sounded mighty thankful that I was going away. There must really be something after all, but what it all meant I was powerless to guess and the effort was making my headache worse.

Guennola had a little sleep, while I sat beside her, trying to read. But my thoughts were just going around and around. When she woke up she didn't seem much better, so I persuaded her to undress and get into bed properly, telling her that I would ask Kérity to bring our suppers up on a tray.

It seemed such a pity that the festive day was ending so badly, and I wished the storm would break so that perhaps there would be more air and a less menacing atmosphere. I busied myself before supper by finishing Guennola's packing, which the old woman had started earlier. Then I left Guennola briefly while I went to my own room and packed most of my possessions, leaving out only my night things and toilet necessities.

It was sad that I would sleep only once more in the room I had grown to love.

Guennola didn't eat much supper, but she said she wasn't sleepy, so I read to her for a short while. Kérity arrived presently with her nightly milk and stood over her while she drank it. Guennola complained that it wasn't hot enough, but, making faces, she drank it. Then I drew the curtains and left her.

We had had supper early and it was still light, though there was no sun at all. I felt increasingly restless and longed to be outdoors. I wondered where Sebastien was, but there was no sign of him as I left the château and made my way down to the lower rocks.

Even when the tide was up it was always possible to circle the island, if one was sure-footed. And, after so much scrambling with Guennola in search of unusual shells, I knew the way exactly. There was only one really difficult place, where one had to scramble down to the old harbor below the sea gate and then up the other side.

The harbor was in deep shadow when I reached it and the water slapped against the stones. It was an eerie place, somehow, on that lowering evening, and I climbed on hurriedly until I was on the western side of the island.

It was rapidly growing darker and thunder was rumbling far away. The château brooded high above me, looking, for once, wholly sinister. I wasn't enjoying being out and I didn't want to go back. I grew more unhappy with every moment and I longed for Sebastien. When I found him, I told myself, I was going to tell him the whole story and ask him to make sense of it for me. For one thing seemed clear; if someone was gunning for him then he must be a danger to someone. He could not be on the side of any villains. Pierre Doumenjou and one of the stonemasons (the one called Gaston) had both been in Port Guenil. One or both of them could have seen us walk toward the stones; they could have reached the wood somehow without us being aware of it. The stonemasons! But they really were working on the roof of the cellar.

It was very still, unnaturally so. Every sound seemed magnified. Over in Port Guenil there was still music, and, nearer at hand, I could hear a baby crying in one of the cottages.

I climbed slowly upward toward the nearest cottages. But I was tired and the way was steep. I suddenly sank down in a hollow and sat with my arms clasping my knees, gazing at the rising water. And then I heard the sound of boots striking the rocks somewhere above me and the clear clink of cups being put down. The nearest cottage was the one occupied by the stonemasons, and I knew there was a bench by the backdoor as well as at the front. The three must be going to sit there to drink their coffee.

Then one of them made a remark in the Breton language, followed by a loud laugh. The words, incredibly, sounded like:

"—a fortune on your boots, man!"

Another voice said something about being careful, because the stuff did stick rather.

Cautiously I raised one eye above the rocks and saw them there, and two of them were examining the third's footwear. Gaston ran his finger along the sole and then held it up, squinting at it.

I ducked down again, completely uncomprehending. They were talking on, quite quietly, but most of their words reached me on that breathlessly still evening. I was already curious and I listened with frowning concentration. Only some words were understandable, yet I suddenly began to build up a terrifying picture.

"Our Monsieur Pierre doesn't trust his brother the

Comte, it seems. Thinks he'll back out before we can get the stuff away. That's why he's made this plan—to hold the kid in a safe place as a hostage."

"But I don't like it. A kid! Oh, he's a deep one. *He* doesn't mean to spend the rest of his life in South America, whatever he's told his brother. I'm having nothing to do with it tonight."

"You don't have to. He'll get Guennola himself. He slipped something in her drink. She'll never wake until she's in that place he knows of on the mainland. I'm going along, too, but he'll manage the boat himself and then

take her in his car. Tomorrow night it'll all be over. We'll get the stuff away and no one will ever know it's been here. The boat will come into the old harbor—"

Though it was so hot and airless, I was very cold. I was actually shivering. I report the conversation like this, because it is easiest, but I didn't get it quite that way. I wasn't wholly sure I had gotten it at all, yet I was in no doubt that Guennola was going to be in danger that night. I was in no doubt, either, that there really was a mystery. That something had been brought to the château, as Sara had said, and that the Comte and his brother were involved. Where Sebastien came into it I still didn't know. It was all so terrible that I seemed frozen to the rock.

I saw Guennola make a face as she drank her milk. Not hot enough. So had Kérity left it somewhere for a short while? Long enough for Pierre Doumenjou to slip something into it? She was getting old and, I knew, was a trifle absent-minded.

In every way, as I crouched there, I was shaken to the heart. Some criminal thing was going on, and the Comte, that seemingly respectable man, was involved. Though I thought they had said that Pierre Doumenjou didn't trust his brother. That was why he was going to make doubly sure, by taking Guennola.

Danger to Guennola—that was the first and most important thing. The rest could wait; I could scarcely face the sure knowledge that everything had been true, that Sara had not used her imagination.

I had to get away without them seeing me. Darkness was coming rapidly and the west was piled with sulphurous clouds. It was a horrible evening and Mont Saint-Hilaire suddenly seemed a horrible place.

I felt more alone than ever before in my life. I wished

quite violently that I had never allowed curiosity to bring
me to Brittany. I had grown so involved with them all.
I had to get away. I had to think. I had to save Guennola.

They might stay on the bench for a long time; I had to
risk it. If I stayed below the rocks and crept along I could
retreat the way I had come. The sea gate would probably
be locked, but I might still find light enough to take me
back to the eastern side of the island. Then I could enter
by the main gate.

I began to move, to edge my way over the rocks. And
suddenly I slipped on a patch of moss, missed my footing
altogether and crashed into a hollow full of small stones.
And of course they heard, on that still evening. As I
picked myself up, rubbing my scraped elbow, dazed, sick,
and bewildered, I saw three suspicious faces looking down
at me. I gasped in English:

"I fell. I was looking for shells for Guennola." Then,
remembering that they probably could not understand, I
repeated it in French.

They helped me up the rocks. There was nothing else
for it, and it was, in fact, a relief not to have to make the
hazardous journey in the growing darkness. I thanked them
as prettily as I could—long afterward I was able to admire
my comparative calm—and walked away around the cottage. I was wearing rubber-soled shoes, and so I was able
to pause. They were talking in Breton again:

"—only the English girl. She couldn't have understood
a word."

And that was the moment when I realized how wonder-
fully I had protected myself, and Guennola, by keeping
my knowledge of the language a secret.

I started to climb the steps toward the gate in the ramparts. And then I heard footsteps behind me. A voice called urgently:

"Gwenda! Gwenda!"

I spun around, scarcely able to believe my ears. For it was Anatole's voice.

Night of Terror

THERE WAS STILL LIGHT enough to see Anatole hurrying up the steps. He looked like a figure from another world in his good Paris clothes.

He was the last person on earth I wanted to see when I so urgently had to think. My face must have expressed a good deal of what I was thinking and feeling, for he stopped a short way below me and demanded:

"What's the matter, Gwenda? Aren't you pleased to see me?"

"Of course," I babbled. "Of course, Anatole. But what on earth are you doing here?"

"I might ask you what you are," he said. He was a little breathless.

I remembered that he had thought I was in London with my family.

"Oh, I changed my mind," I said, still babbling. "I heard at the last minute that my father and mother were going to Canada. I wanted to see Brittany, and then, when I got here, I landed a holiday job. Looking after the little girl at the château."

"So Miss Pritchard told me," he said, a trifle grimly.

Miss Pritchard! Curse the woman. She must somehow

have found out and she was a romantic soul. She was almost the only one who really approved of Anatole. I had never dared to confess to *her* that I had fallen out of love.

"But why did you come?" I demanded. "I'll be back in Paris in a few days. I might even be back there tomorrow." And, speaking very rapidly, I told him about Guennola going to stay with the Doumenjous near the Bois de Boulogne. He immediately looked pleased.

"Excellent. Then I can drive you back. We'll let the little girl go by train, as arranged. Thank God that I haven't to stay here in this outlandish place!"

"Where *are* you staying?" I demanded. Still far away, the thunder rumbled. The whole island looked grim beyond belief.

He passed his hand over his forehead. He looked very hot.

"In a cottage here, down by the harbor. The woman said she could put me up for a night or two. I couldn't find a place in Port Guenil. Some festival or other. I was late arriving, because the car broke down. I borrowed my father's."

It was all increasingly like a nightmare. I just had no room in my mind for Anatole.

"I must go," I said. "Guennola isn't very well."

"Surely she's in bed at this hour?"

"Yes, but—"

"Gwenda, I haven't seen you for a long time. I thought I'd get a better welcome than this."

Why on earth should he have thought so? I hadn't told him I was going to Brittany. He must be hopelessly insensitive. But somewhere in my troubled mind the old guilt was starting. He looked so hurt, and so extraordi-

narily out of place with the surroundings. I thought of
Sebastien in his fishing clothes and my heart was wrung
with longing.

In any case, I *had* to escape.

But Anatole was taking my arm.

"What's it been like? It looks a grim place. Come and
walk by the harbor for a little. The storm won't come up
yet."

I wished it would. He wouldn't want to get those good
clothes wet. But I found myself obediently descending
the steps. There were lights in some of the cottages; a
radio was playing loudly.

Then, as we neared the gap between the cottages that
led to the harbor, Sebastien suddenly appeared. He was
alone and for a moment he didn't seem to see us. Then
he started and his glance flew to Anatole.

"A friend," I gasped. "Anatole, a friend from Paris. He's
on holiday; he came to see—Anatole, this is Sebastien
Doumenjou. He's staying at the château. A cousin."

The two young men greeted each other. I could see
that Anatole wasn't pleased. I didn't know what Sebastien
thought. He didn't linger, but went on toward the
château, and I watched his back in despair. My only
chance . . .

"What a disreputable-looking type!" said Anatole, and
I laughed hysterically. Sebastien had changed into his
fishing clothes. He had looked like a pirate, with that bandage on his face.

We walked around the harbor. The boats had gone
now and the dark water slapped sullenly. It looked the
most uninviting place in the world.

"About tomorrow," said Anatole. "What time are you
leaving?"

"Nine o'clock," I said. "But I don't know . . . I can't say now. I hadn't really intended to go back to Paris yet."

"But you shouldn't wander around Brittany all alone. Oh, Gwenda, what's the *matter* with you?"

"I have a headache," I said, with truth. "It's been a strange kind of day. Anatole, I shall have to go now. They lock the gate." I didn't know if they did; probably not. But he must have seen that the château was a fortress.

I got myself away somehow, leaving him to return to the cottage where he was staying. He would probably be horribly uncomfortable there, poor Anatole. Uncomfortable and alien.

Though my head was throbbing violently I almost ran up the steps, through the gate and into the garden. The fragrance of the roses was almost too heavy and there was no sound anywhere. It was by then almost completely dark and there were very few lights in the château.

Somehow I had to have help. I had to tell someone of the danger that threatened Guennola. But whom could I tell? I could try and find the Comte and lay all my cards in front of him. But the very thought made me shrink. How could I tell that man of whom I was in awe that I knew he was engaged in some illegal racket? I still had no idea what it was, of course, except that it didn't seem to be ordinary smuggling. He loved Guennola and certainly he wouldn't wish her to suffer. Suddenly I knew beyond doubt that that was why he was so anxious to get her away. And, if I did tell him, I might not be safe myself. There might actually have been murder done to a fisherman, and Sara *had* fallen down the tower stairs.

If only I could find Sebastien I could probably put my trust in him. Anything else was unthinkable, and there was, in any case, the evidence of the attack (or attacks) made on him. Sebastien knew something; there wasn't the least doubt of it. Sara said he had been there, but not, apparently, with the others, on the night something was brought to the château.

He had often behaved rather strangely, especially on that night he had followed me to the cellars. He had said he was looking for something to eat, but I suddenly remembered that when I passed the kitchens there hadn't been a light or a sound. So perhaps he hadn't even seen me pass, but had been in the cellars for some reason of his own and had then heard me and had quite a scare.

There was one odd thing that also suddenly flashed into my mind. Guennola had said she thought he was visiting a friend in Brest, and, a few days later, the stonemasons had come from there. So had he gone to see them, to make arrangements?

But it was nonsense. I knew by then that I loved Sebastien and I didn't believe I had fallen in love with a criminal. So it was either a coincidence or he had been investigating on his own account.

Most of these thoughts went through my mind as I stood in the hall at the foot of the stairs. The whole place was terribly silent; the only sound was the thunder rumbling in the distance. I *had* to find Sebastien! So I wandered around, turning on a few lights and then turning them off again. He was not in the sitting room used by the family; it was dark and deserted. The Comte and his wife, and possibly Sebastien, seemed to have gone to bed.

I didn't know where Sebastian slept. The château was so enormous: there were so many rooms, some of which I had probably never seen. He might be anywhere. I was sure that he was nowhere near Guennola and me.

Two of the cats followed me in my restless wandering. In a way they were company. I found the whole place very eerie. I wondered how I had ever enjoyed living there. I was dreadfully afraid, yet one thing was clear. If I could only keep Guennola safe during the night, we were leaving in the morning. The launch was ordered for nine o'clock and after that we would be safe. I might never know what had been going on on the island, unless Sebastien told me some day. Most of me didn't even *want* to know. Perhaps ignorance would be better, for I could never tell the police or anything like that. I owed the Comte something just because he was Guennola's grandfather. It wasn't my business—all I had to do was to go away in the morning and see that the child came as well.

In the end, having given up the search, I looked in at Guennola and found her deeply asleep and breathing heavily. I was sure that she was drugged. I left her door wide open and, still followed by the cats, went along the corridor to my room. It, at least, looked comfortingly familiar, and Kérity had left my cold milk there, as usual, with a plate of cookies.

As I moved around the room I listened for any sound. I couldn't undress and go to bed; I had to be alert. But I was surprised to find that I was hungry. I took a bite of a cookie and unscrewed the top of the flask. One of the cats jumped on the bed and put out a paw and the sudden movement affected my already unsteady hands. The flask fell to the floor and a pool of milk spread over the polished boards.

The cats were lapping eagerly in a moment, while I looked on ruefully. Anyway, I still had the cookies. I sat on the bed, munching slowly, a prey to every terrible thought and still listening for any sound. But the only noise I heard was the approaching thunder. How easy, during a thunderstorm, to pick up a sleeping child and carry her down to a waiting boat. I was sure that most of the fisherfolk of Mont Saint-Hilaire were already in bed, but surely Pierre Doumenjou would take no risks by attempting it early. There might be one or two young men and girls who had stayed over in Port Guenil.

Suddenly I stared in astonishment, for the cats were behaving very strangely. The ginger one, my particular favorite, was yawning widely and staggering a little. The other one slipped on the smooth floor, then made her way to a rug and sank down.

Were they ill? The ginger one hadn't even reached the rug. She was lying on her side, looking very limp. And then the truth hit me. They were drugged. They had drunk most of the milk meant for me.

After a few moments of horror, the knowledge galvanized me into action. Leaving my light on, I went softly along the corridor and into Guennola's room. I could stay there with her behind a locked door. But her bed was small, while mine was large, and to lock her door would only arouse suspicion. It would be much more natural for the stranger in the vast château to lock her door, though I had never done it before.

As I gathered the sleeping child up in my arms I heard the rain starting to fall and the thunder rumbling much nearer. If anyone asked in the morning I could say that I had thought she would be afraid of the storm. It was a blessing in disguise. In every way fate had protected me.

My bedroom light was a beacon in the dark corridor, in which I had not dared to switch on any bulb. I was surprised at how heavy Guennola was and it was a relief to lay her carefully on my bed. Then I shut my door and

turned the big, old key. That ought to be enough; Pierre
Doumenjou would not dare to risk making much noise.
But on second thought, after a glance around at the furniture, most of which was much too heavy to move, I managed to slide a small chest against the door.

Then I went back to the bed and looked down anxiously
at the child. She seemed very hot and her face was flushed.
She was still breathing noisily, but I didn't really suppose
she had been given too much of the drug. Her uncle
merely wanted to keep her as a hostage, not to kill her.
But I would watch her all night to make sure.

There were now great blue flashes of lightning and the
rain was falling in a noisy curtain. The thunder crashed
continuously.

I drew up a chair by the bed and prepared for a long
vigil, for it was not yet ten-thirty. I wondered if there
was a chance that Kérity or perhaps the Comte would go
to see if Guennola was all right. But probably not, for I
was the nearest and Kérity, at least, knew I was aware that
the child was afraid of thunder.

I shall never forget that night as long as I live, though
worse was to come later. The storm raged for an hour,
then at last the thunder moved away, though the rain
still fell heavily.

I turned off the light, since it was making my eyes ache,
but in the darkness it was harder to stay awake. I had to
keep on pinching myself and, in the end, I took to re-
peating snatches of verse to myself.

About one o'clock, struggling with the "Quality of
mercy" from *The Merchant of Venice,* I heard someone
trying my door. In an instant I was wide awake, so tense
that my neck felt as though it would break.

The sound came again and then a perfectly audible

curse. I crept cautiously around the bed, not daring to use my flashlight. I stood with my ear close to the key, remembering thankfully how very solid the door was. But it occurred to me suddenly that he might be able to fetch something that would turn the key from the outside. I ought to have removed it.

I waited there rigidly for what seemed hours, but what was probably about ten minutes, but nothing more happened. So I eased out the key very quietly and crept back to my chair.

When an hour had passed and nothing more happened I allowed myself to doze uncomfortably in the chair, feeling that the danger was probably past. But I always jerked awake again in fright.

I saw, around four o'clock, that Guennola was sleeping more naturally. She was still hot, but her breathing was normal. Once she stirred and spoke a few words, perhaps aware of the beam from my flashlight.

Then I went to glance at the cats, which I had moved onto a rug in a corner. They were warm and still limp, but certainly not dead. I could feel their sides moving rhythmically.

I took off my dress and lay down beside Guennola. After a while, as though realizing my presence, she turned to me and lay close. She was *much* too hot, but of course it was a warm night. There seemed to be no air at all.

I was never so glad to see the dawn come, though it was a weak, gray dawn, with no promise of sun. In fact there was a thick mist and the rain was still falling softly.

I sat by the window for a while, too tired even to think, then I rose and quietly pushed the chest back into place, in case Guennola should wake. I didn't want to alarm her in any way. Then I inserted the key, turned it, and looked out into the corridor.

Everywhere was deserted and quite silent and the danger must definitely be long past. Fisherfolk, I was sure, rose early. The village and the harbor would already be wide awake.

And in two or three hours we would be in the launch, safely on our way from Mont Saint-Hilaire.

At seven o'clock Guennola awoke and stared around her in puzzlement. By then I had washed very briefly in the bathroom, bobbing out once or twice to make sure my door was still shut, and I was dressed and putting my remaining possessions into my suitcase and rucksack. I had also let out the cats, who departed, still a trifle wobbly.

The dismal light fell on Guennola's face and I couldn't stop myself giving a startled cry.

"Oh, Guennola, your face is covered with *spots!*"

She sat up.

"Gwenda, I feel so awful! And what am I doing here in your room?"

"There was a thunderstorm," I explained. "I thought you'd be frightened if you woke, so I brought you in here. You didn't hear a thing, did you?"

"No-o. I'm glad, I hate the thunderstorms."

I was pulling down her nightdress and examining her chest. She was simply covered with a bright red rash. And then the terrible truth hit me. Fate had been unkind, after all. Guennola had the measles; she couldn't possibly start for Paris or anywhere else.

I sat down with a bump on the bed and stared at her, striving to hide my dismay. For I could not possibly go away and leave her at Mont Saint-Hilaire.

No Escape

I ROSE AND WALKED slowly to the window, trying to think. It really was a miserable morning after so much lovely sunshine. The rain was still falling and the thick mist wreathing about the château entirely hid the view.

I felt drained and exhausted after the dreadful night and certainly in no state to cope with the new problem.

Well, I told myself, the only thing to do was to tell Kérity and then the Comte. I was unlikely to see Guennola's grandmother, as she often didn't get up until noon.

"Come back to your own bed," I said gently to Guennola. "I'll find you a clean, cool nightdress. I'm afraid you really have the measles, though I don't know where you could have caught the germ." I had not heard of anyone else on the island who had recently had the measles.

Guennola sighed.

"Oh, but I feel so ill! And now I shan't be able to go to Paris. Me, I had almost started to look forward to it, for you would have come in a few days."

"You'll have to go later. I shall be there all the rest of the summer." I was bustling her along to her room. She went uncomplainingly and climbed into bed, while I opened her suitcase and took out a pink nightdress that was on the very top.

After that I went to the kitchen, seeing no one on the way. There was a delectable smell of coffee and hot rolls and I realized that I was weak with hunger as well as tiredness.

Kérity took the news philosophically. Of course she didn't know that there was any urgent reason for getting the child away.

"She'll have to stay in bed in a darkened room," she said. "With plenty to drink. No doubt the doctor will come over later, but I well know how to nurse a case of the measles. But you, mademoiselle, you have been with the infection. That is most unfortunate."

"That's all right," I assured her. "I've had the measles. My sisters caught it two years ago and gave it to me. But, Kérity, time's getting on and we were to be down by the harbor at nine. I shall have to explain to Monsieur le Comte, and he'll have to cancel all the arrangements."

"Monsieur Sebastien was taking you to Quimperlé. Monsieur le Comte arranged that last night. Monsieur Sebastien has had his breakfast, though actually he had only coffee. And Monsieur le Comte the same. I think the doctor should see him as well. He looks a very sick man to me. In fact, I don't know what's the matter with everyone this morning." Her wrinkled old face was troubled.

I told Kérity that I would have my coffee and rolls upstairs with Guennola, but first I must find Sebastien or Monsieur le Comte. That was easier said than done, for I couldn't find either of them anywhere. The château seemed very dark on that gloomy morning and a feeling of unease was mounting in me every minute. My head ached and my legs ached with climbing the stairs. All I really wanted was a long, peaceful sleep.

Finally, as I was returning down the main staircase, Sebastien came in through the open front door. He wore a raincoat and his hair was wet. We stared at each other for a few moments, then he said:

"The boat will be there at nine. The tide will be just high enough. And my uncle wants me to drive you to Quimperlé. What on earth's the matter, Gwenda?"

"We can't go," I said and poured out the news. I longed to tell him about the dangers of the night as well, but he didn't give me time.

"Then you'd better tell my uncle at once. He'll be most upset. I know he was anxious for Guennola to go."

"I was going to tell him, but I can't find him," I said. "He wasn't in the office or in their sitting room."

"Have another look in the office. Maybe he's there now."

Obediently I made my way there and heard a voice behind the closed door, then the sound of the telephone being hung up. I knocked and, after a few moments, the door opened.

The Comte looked worse than ever, as though he hadn't slept, either. But he spoke pleasantly, as he gestured me into the room.

"You came to say good-bye? And I must also see Guennola. Her grandmother is still in bed, but she's awake and will want to see her before she goes."

"That's just it. We can't go," I gasped, and he stared at me blankly.

"Can't go? But you *must* go! It's all arranged."

I explained about the measles and was horrified to see that he seemed to sag. But on the surface he remained comparatively calm.

"How very unfortunate. Yes, of course the doctor must

come over later, but Kérity will know what to do. She's good with sickness. And you—you'll wish to leave as arranged?"

"No," I said. "I—Please don't ask me to go when Guennola is ill. I think it would upset her."

"Perhaps so," he agreed, looking at me with an expression I couldn't read. "It's very good of you, mademoiselle. I don't think I should ask it of you. In fact—"

I didn't give him time to finish.

"I'm going to have my breakfast in Guennola's room," I said and got myself away. One side of me desperately wanted to escape, but I knew it was out of the question.

I felt frightened and puzzled, for he looked as though the world was ending. I wondered if he knew something about the danger Guennola had been in and might still be in. I didn't know how he could.

On my way back to the kitchen I met two of the stonemasons going along to the cellars, and they wished me good morning. I mumbled something and went on, but I knew that they had stopped and were staring after me. I could feel their gaze boring into my back.

Kérity had my tray ready and also a cold drink for Guennola. I was mounting the side stairs with it when there was a footfall above, and I looked up to see Pierre Doumenjou blocking my way. I nearly dropped the tray.

"Good morning, Mademoiselle Gwenda," he greeted me. "I trust you were not too badly disturbed by the storm?"

I kept my presence of mind somehow.

"Oh, it was awful!" I said girlishly. "I hadn't gone to bed when it started. I knew poor Guennola would be scared, so I took her into my bed. After that I didn't hear a thing!" For he would expect me to have been drugged.

"I'm glad of that," he said, still not moving out of my way.

"And now, just fancy, Guennola has the measles. She's simply covered with spots. She can't go to Paris, of course."

"We-ell!" he said. "The poor child! That is most unfortunate."

"Yes," I agreed, and managed to pass him. I was conscious of him staring after me, but I hoped I had sounded convincing about the storm. If he didn't believe me there was only one other explanation he could find, for the three men might have told him about the conversation I had overheard. But they had no idea I could understand the language, and he couldn't possibly guess, either. There was also the point that he seemed to be the boss, so perhaps they didn't tell him everything.

Later, when I'd had time to think, I would have to tell someone—Sebastien—or even face the Comte again.

Nine o'clock came and Guennola was sleeping. It was darker than ever and still misty and I could hardly stay awake myself. My eyelids felt heavy and my whole body ached. I curled up in the big chair and must have dozed, for when I looked at my watch it was nearly ten o'clock and the door was opening.

I leaped to my feet when I saw that it was the Comte. He put his finger to his lips, as he pushed the door quietly shut behind him.

"She is sleeping? Now, Mademoiselle Gwenda, I want you to do something for me. You're a good girl, and, I'm sure a brave girl. I didn't mean you to be here, but since you are—I want you to stay with Guennola in this room.

And keep the door locked, whatever happens. Will you do that?"

"Why, yes. But—" I stared up into his face, but I wasn't sure that he really saw me. "Monsieur," I said desperately, "I *must* speak to you."

"Later," he said. "Later. Just stay here." And then he was gone.

I was left standing there, hearing the soft whisper of the rain beyond the open window and the quiet breathing of the child. I didn't understand. Something was going to happen, some great danger. And the Comte knew and was ready. But what it could be I had no idea.

Well, if I was going to have to wait all morning with Guennola I had better fetch some things from my room. The Comte couldn't mind that. So I went out into the deserted corridor and along to my room. There I collected my handbag, my radio, and a book I was in the middle of reading.

I didn't wait to make my bed, but hurried back to Guennola's room. I shut the door and put up my hand to turn the key, but it wasn't there. It *must* be there! It was one of the huge old keys and only the evening before I had knocked my arm against it. I had a small purple bruise to prove it.

I searched all over the floor and even looked out in the corridor. No key. And there was no bolt.

In a rising panic, beset by the unknown, I rushed back to my room. Perhaps my own key would fit. But that had gone, too. And then I knew beyond a doubt who had taken them—Pierre Doumenjou, who had no intention of finding any locked doors a second time. He could have taken Guennola's during the night and mine when I was downstairs. The Comte must simply have taken it for granted there was a key. I was sure he hadn't looked.

I stood in Guennola's room and looked around. Most of the furniture was far too heavy to move and there was only the old armchair. It was comfortable, but quite light in weight. It wouldn't block the door for more than a few moments.

I should have to risk leaving Guennola to find the Comte; there was no other way, because, though there had once been bells in each room, they no longer worked. Kérity had told me that soon after my arrival.

I must explain to the Comte that I couldn't lock us in, and, at the same time, I *must* find out why he had wished it. I had to tell him I had some knowledge, though so vague, about what was going on at the château.

I went out into the corridor again and stood listening so intently that I felt a stab of pain in my head. Far away, in the depths of the château, there was a banging sound. So it seemed that the stonemasons were at least making a pretense of getting on with the work. But what other work was there? I couldn't imagine what their real purpose on the island could be.

The rest of the château was wrapped in utter and very frightening silence. I longed for anyone, even for Kérity or the ancient Guildas—any human soul. Most of all I wanted Sebastien. I didn't remotely understand where he fitted into it all, but I had to talk to him more urgently than ever. Even more than that I just wanted his presence.

In my whole life I had never felt so terribly alone, not even during those first days in Paris. Alone and puzzled and scared, not only for myself but for Guennola. If she had been just any child I would have felt something, but during the time I had been with her I had grown very fond of her, almost as though she were an extra little sister.

I wondered if it would be safe to leave her, even for the short while it would take me to find someone. I had my mysterious orders and the Comte was not a man to be disobeyed lightly.

So could I take Guennola into another room that had a key? There were a few shrouded bedrooms near by. But that would mean waking her and probably frightening her very much, and the measles, if wrongly treated, could be quite serious.

"Let her sleep," I told myself, and, still in a state of hopeless indecision, I shut the door and wandered to the window.

Guennola's room was high above the rose garden and the main entrance to the château. In fine weather there was a superb view over the ramparts to the harbor and the mainland coast. Now, though the rain seemed to have stopped, mist still shrouded the island. Perhaps it was not quite so thick. I could at least see the rosebeds and the great gate.

I stood between the partly closed curtains, by the open window. And suddenly I saw that the little gate in the big one was opening slowly. I watched, hoping that it might be Sebastien.

But it was Anatole who came slowly into the garden, who stood there, looking around him in a puzzled, uncertain way.

Anatole! During all that had happened I had never given him another thought. I had totally forgotten his unwelcome presence at Mont Saint-Hilaire.

Morning of Terror

HE LOOKED SO ALIEN and, at the same time, so ordinary. He had always looked conventional for a student, and those good city clothes just had no place at Mont Saint-Hilaire.

I watched in a kind of daze as he advanced slowly along the broad path between the roses. He looked like a tourist waiting to be shown around a château in the Loire valley.

I must, I thought, be a little hysterical, and no wonder. But he was looking for me, wondering why we had never arrived at the harbor at nine. He would never believe that I had forgotten all about him—he would never believe anything.

I leaned out of the window. He was already almost out of sight, where the rose garden became the courtyard in front of the main steps.

"Anatole!" I called. Or I *meant* to call. I realized, after a moment, that his name had been merely a croak and that he couldn't possibly have heard, so far below.

And now he had gone, presumably up the front steps. I could imagine him in the hall, staring around him, wondering how it was possible for people still to *live* in such a place.

wondering how it was possible for people still to *live* in such a place.

And then I heard shouts down by the harbor, followed by a crack that sounded like a gunshot. But of course it couldn't be.

Yet I found myself standing rigid, staring at the gate. Anatole had shut the little door behind him, but—after perhaps two or three minutes had passed—it suddenly burst open. I recognized Gaston, the stonemason I liked least. He slammed the gate behind him and seemed to be wrestling with the medieval bolts. He was using only one hand and there was a great sense of urgency about him.

Then he turned and I saw that his left arm was hanging by his side in rather a strange way. He gave a frantic look around, then, clasping his right hand over his other arm, he began to run toward the château. In a few moments he had disappeared, presumably up the front steps.

Now I really was scared, though of course I still didn't understand. I hesitated, then went to the door and opened it. I heard nothing so I returned to the window. The air was very still and I could hear feet on the steps that led up from the village—excited voices. Then someone giving what seemed to be orders.

Almost at once there were sounds by the gate. Someone was trying to open it, though I was sure that Gaston had fastened all the great, ancient bolts. Now there was banging, urgent, loud. A commanding voice shouted in French:

"Open the gate!"

And then someone appeared in the courtyard, running along the path between the roses. It was one of the other stonemasons. As I watched, still frozen there at my high window, he took up a stance with his back to the gate,

and he held a gun in his right hand, pointing straight toward the château. He only had to raise it to shoot me. I shrank back in the folds of the curtains.

It all seemed quite unreal, but some part of me realized the danger.

"Open! Open at once!" The shouts and thudding were much louder.

The man with the gun yelled back:

"I'm armed! You won't get in this way. And there's someone armed at the sea gate, too!"

Held at the window in the folds of the heavy curtains, I had forgotten about the unlocked door. And suddenly it burst open. For a moment, entangled in the draperies, I couldn't turn and see what was happening. When I did, I saw Pierre Doumenjou bending over the bed, gathering up Guennola, wrapped in a blanket, in his arms.

When I rushed at him he turned neatly, flinging her over his shoulder. A gun flashed out in his right hand.

"You will keep away, mademoiselle, if you value your safety. I'm taking the child. With her for protection we may yet get away."

"But she's ill. You'll kill her!" I knew that Guennola was awake. She cried:

"Gwenda! Help me!"

"Keep out of it!" Pierre Doumenjou snapped. "If you want to stay alive . . ."

He had left the door open and now he marched through it. I caught a glimpse of Guennola's terrified face. There was a heavy old vase on a chest. Scarcely knowing what I was doing, I picked it up and rushed to the door. I aimed carefully and it hit him behind the right knee, almost knocking him to the floor.

I ducked back, expecting a shot, but it never came. He strode away along the corridor and disappeared down the side stairs.

Then I screamed. I yelled for Monsieur le Comte, for

Sebastien, for Kérity, for anyone. And Monsieur le Comte came. His face was gray, but there was an air of excitement about him. He looked more alive than I had yet seen him.

"I told you to stay behind a locked door!" he shouted, as he approached.

"I couldn't . . . Your brother stole the key. And my key," I gasped. "Oh, what's happening? He has taken Guennola!"

He stopped then, and the excitement went out of him. "Oh, *mon Dieu!*" he whispered. Then: "The police have come. They've surrounded the island, but somehow the men were informed."

"One of them came back from the harbor and locked the gate," I stammered. "I think he was shot in the arm. But oh, monsieur! Why have the police . . . How did they know?"

"I *asked* them to come," he said. "I had to do it soon or it would have been too late. I thought you and Guennola would be gone."

I didn't have time to ask any questions, because he was already disappearing toward the main stairs. He shouted over his shoulder:

"You'd better keep out of the way! They all have guns, I think, and I haven't a single firearm that works."

But how could I keep out of the way? Guennola had been my responsibility and I had let Pierre Doumenjou take her. I plunged down the side stairs and soon heard shouting and banging from the kitchen. It seemed as though Kérity and her young assistant had been locked in.

I rushed along the passage, heading toward the main part of the building. Just as I approached the door that shut the kitchen quarters off from the hall I stumbled over

something and gave a stifled scream. The passage was
dark, but in a few moments I realized that it was Anatole,
lying there inert.

Anatole! In the excitement and terror that had immediately followed his entrance I had again forgotten all
about him.

I dropped on my knees beside him, thinking for a few
horrified moments that he was dead. But he was warm
and breathing, though quite unconscious. I moved my
hands over him, dreading to feel the stickiness of blood,
but all I found was an already rising bump on his head.
Someone had knocked him out, and one side of me
thought perhaps it was a good thing. What could Anatole
possibly do to help in such an appalling situation?

Anatole would probably live to tell the tale—and what
a tale he would make if it! But there seemed nothing I
could do for him then and I was frantic to know where
Guennola was.

I burst out through the door that led into the hall and
found the Comte there, shielded by the open front door.
I rushed toward him and he spun around as though expecting an attack, which indeed he probably was. I was
sorry I had alarmed him, when things were already so bad.

"For God's sake, mademoiselle!" he cried. "Go back
upstairs and keep out of this."

But I had seen out into the courtyard. Pierre Doumenjou had joined the stonemason by the gate in the ramparts.
He still held Guennola over his left shoulder and the gun
was in his other hand, pointing straight toward us. As I
stared in horror, he raised his voice and called:

"You there! Police! I have the child, so you'd better take
care. I'm armed, and I shan't hesitate to shoot her."

There was silence at first from behind the gate, then an authoritative voice called:

"You haven't a hope of getting away. Don't add murder to your other iniquities. Open the gate and come quietly."

"Never!" Pierre Doumenjou's voice had a wild ring in it. I was sure he was insane.

The Comte stood quite motionless, but his lips were moving. I thought that he was praying.

I tried to think. Four men. One stonemason was at the sea gate, but where was the wounded one? And where was Sebastien in all this terror and danger?

"Sebastien?" I whispered, and the Comte answered me:

"I think still outside the ramparts . . . I told him this morning. He went down to meet the police. We hoped to take them all by surprise, but something went wrong."

So it was the Comte and I and . . .

"Madame la Comtesse?" I gasped.

"Still in bed. She knows nothing. Or, at least, perhaps she suspects all isn't well. But this . . . maybe she'll hear nothing. Sometimes she falls asleep again."

The Comte and I. The château was a fortress. The Comte and I against four armed and desperate men.

"Two here," I said, "and one at the sea gate. We have to know where the other man is. The wounded one."

"It can make no difference," said the Comte.

"But it might." I had forgotten to be in awe of him; we were in it together. "Look!"

For the big, broad-shouldered stonemason had taken a step nearer Pierre Doumenjou and they were arguing fiercely, in low voices. The big man was waving his hands about and the gun nearly caught Pierre Doumenjou on the ear.

"I don't think he really likes your brother very much," I said. "I believe he has a conscience about some things, even if he is some kind of crook." For I was pretty sure he was the one who had been upset at the idea of kidnaping Guennola.

"I'm going to make sure where the other one is," I added, after a moment.

I went back across the hall and along the kitchen passage toward the cellar stairs. The knocking in the kitchen had stopped, but I could hear wailing and crying.

The light was burning over the cellar stairs. I went slowly down them, calling: "It's me, Gwenda! Is anyone there?"

I might have been shot, but I wasn't. There was only total silence. And the injured man was lying at the foot of the steps, white-faced and still, with blood seeping out of a wound in his arm, just above the elbow. He had warned the others and then collapsed. His face was very white and he seemed to have lost a lot of blood. I didn't think he was much of a danger, but, just to make sure, I searched his pockets. My fingers closed on a gun and I removed it gingerly. Perhaps the Comte knew how to shoot, even if he didn't have any workable firearms.

Looking back, I am amazed at how calm I was. But probably I was dazed and in an unreal world. I only knew that we were imprisoned with desperate, wicked men and that Guennola was in the worst danger of all.

On the way back I unlocked the kitchen door and found Kérity, the young girl, whose name was Julie, and Guildas —all, apparently, more or less paralyzed with terror. It was Julie who was wailing. She was sitting at the kitchen table with her head on her arms, but she jerked upright when she heard me.

"What is it?" the old man gasped. "Who locked us in? Both doors . . . And the windows too high to climb out of. We heard someone yelling that he had been shot and the police were coming—"

"They've come," I said. "But they can't get in. There are armed men holding both gates. If you take my advice you'll all stay here."

I realized that they were all staring at me with stupefied expressions and looked down at the gun that I held in my hand.

"I took it off the wounded one," I explained. "I thought it might help."

"Guennola?" cried Kérity.

"He's got her—her uncle. He's wicked, desperate. Crazy, I think. And he's armed. They're all armed. Keep away. Stay here."

I heard the ring of authority in my voice and was dimly surprised. Then I went back to the hall and the front door. The Comte had gone, then I saw him out in the courtyard, walking steadily between the roses. He seemed unafraid of the guns that were pointing straight at him.

"Pierre, this is madness!" he called. "Would you kill a child? Kill me, if you must, but let the child go back to bed."

Pierre Doumenjou laughed. He really looked insane.

"Kill *you!* I'd like nothing better, and maybe I will presently. But you can suffer a little longer. I always hated you. And we owe this to you. I might have known you weren't to be trusted. You told the police and you thought your precious Guennola would be safely away. But we'll beat you all yet. We'll get away and possibly some of the stuff with us."

Then he lifted his head and shouted:

"You will agree to give us safe conduct to the harbor, or I'll shoot the child!"

He *must* be insane. Even if they could get to a boat and away, they would soon be picked up. But he was counting on the safety that Guennola's presence would give.

From behind the ramparts there was silence. Then the same voice we had heard before shouted:

"You can't get away or get any of the stuff away. It's finished, Doumenjou. Give up the child and surrender."

Pierre Doumenjou shouted something back, but I wasn't listening. I was retreating away from the door. There were several other ways out into the garden and surrounding courtyards, and I didn't want to be seen. I could see no way to rescue Guennola, but I might think of something and there was just no point in being shot.

I paused for a moment to look down at Anatole. He was still out; still peacefully unaware of what was happening. I wished I had something to put under his head, but there was nothing.

I opened one of the heavy old side doors and stepped out into the soft, damp misty air. I was out of sight around a tower, but the great front gate was not far away. Here there were still some roses and, in a corner, several trees.

As I stood there, shaking, sick, but ready to be resolute if I had an idea, I heard a sound in the branches of the old tree that reached to the top of the ramparts and even higher. Perhaps a bird. But a branch was moving and the tree seemed to be straining.

A few moments later, with incredulous relief, I saw Sebastien's face appear over the ramparts. Then, after a short struggle, he disappeared among the leaves.

Seconds later I saw him again, climbing slowly and quietly down.

"Sebastien!" I whispered. My heart was racing with sudden hope. "How on earth did you manage—"

He gave me a startled look as he slid to the ground.

"Oh, Gwenda! What a scare you gave me. And why *that*? Can you use it?"

"The gun? No." I stared at it, then raised my eyes to his. "I took it from the wounded man. I was going to give it to the Comte, but he's out there in the garden by the gate, trying to talk to his brother."

"My dear, dear girl!" For a moment he put his hands on my shoulders. "Are you all right? I got a good thick rope and managed to throw it up. Took me ages to get it over a branch. These ramparts weren't meant to be climbed, but I'm a mountaineer, remember. They didn't know the technique in olden times."

"But the police . . . Do they know?"

"They know. I volunteered. I was frantic to get inside. I'm armed, too." He patted his pocket. "It seemed the only chance."

"But he's holding Guennola, there by the gate. There's nothing we can do. At the slightest move he'll shoot her."

"We'll have a good try," he said grimly. He was very white and looked tense. "Where are they all?"

"One by the sea gate, one by the front gate, with Pierre Doumenjou, one in the cellar, unconscious and bleeding." He gave me an astonished look. "Well," I said, "I went to look. He's by the cellar steps. There's just one chance, perhaps. I don't think that big man likes the way things are going. He's holding the main gate, but—"

"Michel?"

"Is that his name? I don't think he's a murderer by nature. Sebastien, I'll do anything! It's my fault. I should have guarded Guennola better, but he took the key."

"I don't know yet what we can do," he said. "But you

mustn't get into any danger. Keep out of the way. A girl—"

"No," I said. "No, it's my affair too. There must be something we can do. He's insane . . . Pierre Doumenjou. Maybe we can distract his attention."

We peered cautiously around the great tower at the side of the château. The scene in the courtyard and garden was much the same as before, except that, in the gray light, Pierre Doumenjou looked to me to be exhausted. Guennola, though so small for her age, was, as I well knew, no light weight. And he had been holding her for quite a time.

Sebastien looked and then murmured, "Oh, *mon Dieu!*"

He sounded utterly dismayed, but his face was grim and resolute. I felt that things were better now that he was there.

Behind the Ramparts

SEBASTIEN SIGNALED to me and we withdrew.

"The first thing," he whispered, "is to deal with the man at the sea gate."

"And let the police in?" I asked.

"And let the police in. Not that it will do much good while he's holding Guennola out in front. I think she's fainted, by the way, which is the best thing that could happen."

"I shall never forgive myself," I said, looking at him miserably. "I protected her last night, but now—"

"Save it," he said. "We'll talk later, if this thing is ever over. Look, Gwenda, I can see you won't keep out of it—"

"No. I won't hide and do nothing, so it's no use asking me to."

He bent down and gave me a quick kiss on the forehead.

"You English! Then you'd better learn how to use the gun. But don't, for heaven's sake, use it unless you have to. It will simply be a protection for you. I bet you are good at sports?"

"Oh, yes."

"Then you'll know how to aim by instinct, I expect." He told me briefly, clearly, what to do, adding: "But be careful. Don't take any chances. Keep out of the way if you can, otherwise pretend you know all about shooting. It may help."

I nodded and he went on:

"Now the thing is—how am I going to deal with that one at the sea gate? He'll probably be facing this way. Don't make a sound. Rubber-soled shoes?"

"Yes."

He began to move cautiously around the château and I followed. It took quite a while, as it was such a huge place. There were little sunken courtyards, steps, narrow, cobblestoned paths. But at last he was directly behind the building, though keeping out of sight behind a bastion. I knew that he could see the sea gate and I waited, holding my breath. I could feel my heart pounding.

He gave me a small signal and came softly back.

"It's just as I thought. He's facing this way, but very unsettled and not quite knowing what's happening. There are police on the other side. I can hear them talking."

And then we heard raised voices and both of us sped silently toward the bastion. The gunman had turned around and was yelling over the ramparts that they could just hold their tongues. They weren't likely to get in that way. His voice had a troubled, almost hysterical ring.

His back was turned and there were only a few yards between Sebastien and him.

"Oh, no!" I whispered, but Sebastien had gone. He went incredibly fast down the three steps, moving as lightly as a cat. As he raised his gun in his hand the stonemason began to turn. But he was too late. The butt hit him on the side of the head and he crumpled without a sound.

My legs were shaking so much that I could hardly stand. For a split second I had thought that Sebastien would be shot. But he was very much alive; he was pushing back the great bolts, working carefully so that no sudden sharp sound might be heard on the still air.

The opened door revealed six policemen with guns drawn, and, behind them, a misty scene. The old harbor was only just visible, but I glimpsed a large white boat.

Sebastien gestured to the man at his feet. As he did so, I thought that he looked like some hero of old, even though he wore modern clothes. Then he was speaking, explaining. I went quickly to his side.

The police crowded in. The man in charge was a tall, handsome officer, who seemed to grasp the situation very quickly.

"Still holding the child by the front gate? Then we must use the utmost caution." He turned to give orders to two of his men. They were to take the unconscious man down to the boat and see that he didn't escape.

"And one in the cellar, wounded," I said. "You might get him. But oh, what about Guennola?"

"Mademoiselle has had a terrible time," said the police officer, looking at me searchingly and seeming surprised by the gun in my hand.

"It isn't over," I said. "It doesn't help much that you're here inside. Oh, there must be something that we can do!"

Sebastien and I showed them the various entrances into the château and then the police officer went with Sebastien to peer out through the front door. They seemed to have forgotten me, so I escaped quietly and went to look around the tower. The Comte was still standing in the courtyard and the little tableau by the gate hadn't changed much.

Pierre Doumenjou suddenly shouted to his brother:

"You! Get back into the château if you don't want to die immediately. This has gone on for long enough."

The Comte retreated. I thought he must have gone up the steps, but I couldn't see. Michel was saying something again, gesticulating urgently. He looked desperately unhappy and the gun was no longer held so menacingly. Pierre Doumenjou snapped something in a savage undertone. He looked as though he couldn't hold Guennola another moment.

And I couldn't bear it any longer. All my love for Guennola surged up, coupled with a strange kind of misery. She had had trouble enough, and, even if she did escape this dreadful danger, she might never be the same.

But she had to have the chance of being happy again some day. Whatever it cost. And then I knew what I was going to do. I make no claim to being a heroine; it was guilt that drove me on, because I had not guarded her better. And really I had no time to think. I only knew that there had to be an exchange. *I* would be the hostage and he must release Guennola. Probably he didn't care in the least whom he held; all he must be thinking about now was how to get away.

It wasn't any use shouting out to him. I had to get nearer first and then speak in such a way that he wouldn't shoot. And I must leave my own gun behind.

So I put it carefully down on a narrow ledge of stone, dropped down on my hands and knees, and began to crawl among the roses. The earth was very wet and it had a sharp acrid smell. Thorns caught at my dress and hair, but I made progress. I was getting nearer and nearer the gate and somehow I managed not to shake the bushes. The slightest alarm and he might fire blindly.

Cautiously I raised my head to look. Pierre Doumenjou was turning to shout over the ramparts.

And in that moment I heard a whisper behind me.

"Gwenda! Stop!"

Luckily Guildas did very little gardening and the rose bushes were high and getting out of hand. I turned my head a little in my crouching position and saw Sebastien within touching distance. His face was very white and there was a bad scratch on his cheek, under the dirty bandage.

His voice was scarcely above a breath.

"You fool! What are you doing?"

"I thought you were in the hall," I mouthed. "Oh, leave me alone, please. He has to take me instead of Guennola."

"He'll take you both. No, darling Gwenda, you aren't going to do that—"

Actually we need not have whispered so very quietly for the shouting had been going on all the time.

I raised my head again to look at Pierre Doumenjou and saw that, while still shouting and with his head partly turned away, he had let Guennola slip to the ground and was holding her against him. And Guennola hadn't sagged; she was standing upright with her bare feet planted on the cold damp stones. I caught one glimpse of her little spotty face, her wide gray eyes. Then she had lifted Pierre Doumenjou's left hand and dug her teeth into it. In another split second she was running—clever child, not straight up the path, where she could have been shot instantly, but into the roses, where she flung herself on her face almost on top of me.

Two shots rang out, then there was utter confusion. People shouting—someone giving orders. I saw Sebastien rise up from the roses, with a smoking gun in his hand, but I really registered none of it. I was sitting on the wet ground, holding Guennola, who was shaking and crying. My hair was painfully caught on some thorns.

"It's all right! It's all right!" Sebastien told me, and he
disentangled my hair and helped us both up. Then he
put the gun in his pocket and took Guennola in his arms.
Somewhere I had a fleeting thought that perhaps the great-
est danger to her now was that she'd die of pneumonia.
The measles, a temperature, and all that exposure to the
damp. But at least it wasn't cold.

The great gate was open, not just the little one. The
courtyard was full of police. They were holding Michel,
who seemed to have no fight in him, and Pierre Doumenjou was lying on the ground.

"I only shot him in the arm," I heard Sebastien explaining.

"One of my men got him as well," said a second police
officer.

The Comte was there, and Kérity, Guildas, and Julie. Huge tears were pouring down Julie's face.

And then two policemen came down the steps holding someone between them. Someone in city clothes, who was protesting violently.

"But I tell you I know nothing about what's going on. Someone hit me. Let me go at once!"

Anatole! Oh, poor Anatole!

"We found him wandering around in a dark passage," said the big man on his right. "Looks as though one of his own chums knocked him out."

It galvanized me into action. Still dazed, sick, and shaking, I ran forward.

"That's a friend of mine, Anatole Lamarche, from Paris. He got into the château just before it all started. I saw him from a window, then forgot. He isn't a criminal. You've made a mistake."

Anatole didn't even seem grateful. Released, he stood rubbing his arms, glaring at everyone, including me.

"I shall require a full explanation and an apology. Is this how you normally treat visitors to Brittany?"

Oh, dear! He even had to be pompous at a time like this.

I began to laugh, then to cry. Dimly I knew that Sebastien was carrying Guennola toward the château. Her voice floated back triumphantly:

"I *bit* him! Hard. I hope it hurt! Is he dead?"

"No," said Sebastien. "I don't think so."

"And now I want to go back to bed!"

Someone was speaking to me, comforting me. It was Monsieur le Comte. And then we were all walking toward the château, except for the men who were taking Michel and Pierre Doumenjou away. It was all over.

Hours later four of us sat in the big sitting room; the Comte, Madame la Comtesse, Sebastien, and I. The sun was shining brilliantly and I could see the great shore.

Anatole had gone back to Paris, still unforgiving. I rather thought I would never see him again. I felt a little guilty about him, of course, partly because I found, in retrospect, that his role in the drama was funny. The memory of his face when he was arrested as a desperate criminal . . . . Oh, poor dear Anatole! I hoped he would soon find a nice, ordinary French girl and live happily ever after. Perhaps he would one day tell his children about the terrible goings-on at the Château of Saint-Hilaire.

Guennola was in bed and in a deep sleep. The doctor had given her an injection and had said that, with careful nursing, she should be all right. It was only a mild case of the measles and the worst aspect was the shock she had suffered. But she had seemed proud of herself. It was almost as though that bite at her uncle's hand had evened all the scores. After all, she had never liked him.

"She used to have spirit," the doctor had said, "before her parents' death. Treat her properly, tell her the whole story as soon as she's well enough, and don't omit anything. She's not a baby, and the truth will be better than half-understood memories. Then get her away from here to Paris and give her something new to think about."

Pierre Doumenjou was dead. He had lived a few hours and had made a full confession, taking all the blame. He had killed a fisherman and had tried to kill both Sara and Sebastien, believing them to be dangerous to his scheme. He had threatened his brother to force him to do as he wished, and he had planned to kidnap Guennola as an extra lever, but had been foiled by a thunderstorm or, he had added, by that English girl, Gwenda. Though how she could have known the plans . . .

I had explained. I had told my story to the police and now I was telling it to the family. And by then, of course, I knew what had been brought to the château on Sara's mysterious night—a load of stolen gold. It had been stolen in Paris and the theft had made the headlines for days, and had often been mentioned on the radio. But there were so many daring thefts and crimes in the news that I had paid little attention to that one. The stonemasons' real job had been to melt the gold down to more manageable proportions and one of the things they had brought in the big crates had been a portable furnace. In a day or two their work would have been finished and the gold would have been taken away to another country. I had had one clue to what they were doing but it had meant nothing to me at the time. That evening I had overheard them talking about the gold on their boots.

"But you mean you can really understand the Breton language?" Sebastien asked.

"Yes, in a strange way. It's almost uncanny. Oh, I never thought when I learned Welsh as a child that it would come in so handy!"

The Comte looked ten times better, and even his wife, though she had had a terrible shock, seemed to be more at rest. It looked as though things might work out all right for them as far as the gold went, though when the "stonemasons" appeared for trial the whole affair would be resurrected. The Comte had already explained his own terrible part in it.

"My brother and I never got along, even when we were boys. He was very jealous of me because I was the elder, and he was such a different character. Forceful, rebellious, and always seeking money and power. I suspected years ago that he had gone outside the law, but I never had any evidence of it until he came to me with his proposition. Of course I refused, even though he offered me a large share in the money. I needed money desperately, but I never even thought of agreeing. But then he threatened me. He swore that if I agreed to their bringing the gold here, even if I stood by my principles and took no money, he would go away to South America and I would never see him again. But if I refused he would see that Guennola never lived to inherit the island. I knew he meant it—he was capable of anything. I suspected he wasn't quite sane."

"Then why," I asked, "did you decide to call the police?"

He looked at me gravely.

"I owe that to you, Mademoiselle Gwenda. When you came I had the feeling, right from the start, that there was some reason for your presence on Mont Saint-Hilaire. It was just instinct until you went to see Sara and the Sister told me you had been alone with her. I always suspected that Sara knew something, and I was afraid that my brother had felt the same and had tried to kill her. I was very much relieved when she went safely away to Vannes. I didn't think he would make another attempt."

"But—"

"You left your handbag on the rocks and—forgive me—I looked inside it. I felt there might be some clue, and I found Sara's letter. I didn't know how it had come into your possession, but I knew for certain you suspected something, and I also knew that Sebastien did. It gave me the necessary courage. I hoped that my brother would be in prison for years and that he would never dare to attack Guennola if the police were forewarned. Any accident to her would immediately be placed at his door."

Later Sebastien and I walked down to the harbor. The

village was quiet, but people looked out at us curiously from the cottages.

"You even suspected me?" Sebastien asked.

"Well, only very slightly. Sara said you were there on that night the gold was brought."

"So I was, but the others didn't know. I couldn't sleep and I realized something was going on. Afterwards Pierre must have guessed I knew something. He always hated my being there. He tried to talk me into going away, but I stuck it out. I didn't know exactly what was going on, but I had a feeling they were smuggling. I meant to save the Comte from being involved if I could."

"And Pierre Doumenjou tried to kill you?"

"It seems so. He knew I'd never be on *his* side."

"And Guennola said you went to Brest. That time you were away for a night or two, just when I arrived. I began to wonder why. I thought perhaps you had gone to see the 'stonemasons.'"

Sebastian looked astonished.

"I didn't go to Brest. I went to Dinan. A friend was in some slight trouble and I thought I ought to go and see him, though I hated to be away just then."

"She said she heard you asking for a Brest telephone number."

"Little Big Ears!" he cried, looking amused. "I remember that. It was about some new tires my uncle had ordered for his car. A complete coincidence although actually I know that none of those three men came from Brest. Two are from a village outside Rennes and the other from Lorient."

"I'm sorry, Sebastien," I said humbly. "Everything was so strange. I never really thought—"

We were right out on the breakwater by then. It was

a wonderful evening after the storm, softly colored and very calm.

Suddenly Sebastien said:

"That friend of yours from Paris—"

"Poor Anatole!" I murmured. Then I told him about the spring and how I had soon realized we were not suited to each other. Sebastien listened gravely.

"Yes, it does seem to be 'poor Anatole.' I can see how he felt about you. But I'm glad he's no longer a rival. We'll meet again in Paris, Gwenda."

He kissed me then, and we didn't care who saw our figures silhouetted against the sunset. I was exhausted, but very happy.

In Paris Again

SIX MONTHS LATER Sebastien and I walked by the river Seine. It was January and Paris was in the grip of frost, but the sun was shining.

We walked on the Ile de la Cité, in the gardens beside the Cathedral of Notre Dame. I wore a red coat and a cap to match and Sebastien was muffled up in a big coat and a blue scarf. Gone was the rakish fisherman, the pirate of Mont Saint-Hilaire, but he looked very handsome and very well and cheerful.

In those six months we had gotten to know each other very well. Just after Christmas he flew with me to London to meet my family, and at that time we became engaged. Mother was a little sorry, she said, that I was marrying a Frenchman, but in spite of that they all loved Sebastien.

"And after all," she added later, "Paris isn't so far away. It's not as though you'd gone to America."

"I've had news of Anatole," I told Sebastien, as we crossed the bridge that led to the Ile Saint-Louis.

Sebastien grinned, looking at me inquiringly.

"He's engaged to a girl named Louise, whose father owns a big store. Mr. Wade says she's a year older than he and plump and plain."

Sebastien laughed.

"You never heard another word from him?"

"No. I believe he told everyone that I must be a wild strange girl to get into such an adventure."

He laughed again.

"I'd sooner have a bit of wildness. But then I'm not Anatole."

"No, thank goodness!" I agreed fervently.

"Don't forget we have to get out to the Bois by four-thirty," Sebastien remarked, as we traversed the whole length of the main street on the Ile Saint-Louis.

"I haven't, but I did want to do some walking first," I said. "I don't get much exercise on weekdays now it's dark so early."

"I wonder how Guennola likes the new flat?" he said thoughtfully.

"Oh, she adores it," I told him. "She telephoned me last night *and* this morning. And she starts at her new day school in two days' time. I'm sure it's best, but I can't really imagine them living anywhere but at Mont Saint-Hilaire."

"It is best. That place was too haunted for Guennola. She's been a different child these last few months."

"I'm glad, at least, that the Comte hasn't sold the island."

As soon as Guennola had recovered from the measles and the shock, she had come to stay with Sebastien and his family, and two or three months later the Comte and his wife had followed, to stay in a hotel. An American film company had decided to make a film on Mont Saint-Hilaire and the money would go a long way toward helping to keep up the place for a few years. But the Comte had decided that it would be better for them all to leave.

So now the château had been rented to a rich French businessman, who wanted to spend a few years of his retirement in some idyllic spot.

Then we walked rapidly toward the nearest Métro station and journeyed toward the Bois de Boulogne. The Comte had taken a very large flat not far from where Sebastien and his family lived, and they had moved in only two days before.

During the months that had passed I had seen a good deal of Guennola. She had had lessons from a visiting governess, but on weekends she had gone out either with me alone or else Sebastien had been there as well. We had taken her to the ballet, the parks, and the art galleries. She was enchanted with Paris and vowed that all she wanted was to be a real Parisian. She was also thrilled by our engagement.

The flat was in a huge old converted house and Guennola opened the door. She looked very different from the nervous child of the summer. She had grown taller and her face was pink with health.

"Sebastien! Gwenda!" she cried. "Oh, you've brought the cold in with you! Isn't this a lovely place? *Grandpère* and *Grandmère* are so happy. And I am happy, too! Kérity likes it also. She says it's a change from the island. She's going to go to the cinema and find all the best places for shopping."

They all looked happy. The Comte was quite upright again and I knew he had started to write a history of Mont Saint-Hilaire. The Comtesse was having some special treatment for her leg and looked much better. The flat was warm and pleasantly furnished and they seemed quite at home sitting by the roaring fire.

But, as they greeted me, I could see behind them that other place. That romantic island, washed by sea and, in winter, probably often stormbound.

I should never forget Mont Saint-Hilaire, and I doubted if they would, either.

Some day, I knew, I would have to go back, if only on a very short visit to Port Guenil. Perhaps Sebastien and I would go that way on our honeymoon in June and see some more of Brittany at the same time.

The Comte was pulling up chairs and Guennola was chattering.

She was happy in Paris; most of the shadows had gone. I wondered if she would ever live on Mont Saint-Hilaire when she was older. But that was up to her and only time would tell.

We settled ourselves by the fire.